Praise for Kim Rees' *Past Lies*

5 Angels "This book drew you into the story and made you want to really experience the things that the characters were going through...?This was a great book and I?ll be checking out more from Kim Rees."

~ *Missy, Fallen Angel Reviews*

4 Nymphs "Past Lies is an emotion filled tale that keeps readers guessing. Betrayal, love and a healthy dose of lust heat the pages as the connection between Zachary and Anna sizzles to a fevered pitch. Ms. Rees delivers a passionate romance with realistic characters and a quirky storyline that makes for an entertaining read."

~ *Water Nymph, Literary Nymphs*

4 Hearts "PAST LIES is a book you simply will not want to put down.?"

~ *Mandie, Loves Romances and More*

4.5 Hearts "This story quickly catches the readers? attention and keeps it as little by little the truth behind the lies is revealed. Past Lies by Kim Rees is a story filled with twist, turns and exciting surprises that make this a story that will entertain the readers."

~ *Anita, The Romance Studio*

Past Lies

Kim Rees

Hi Lisa

Hope you enjoy

*Zach and Anna's
Story*

Kim Rees

A Samhain Publishing, Ltd. publication.

Samhain Publishing, Ltd.
512 Forest Lake Drive
Warner Robins, GA 31093
www.samhainpublishing.com

Editing by Sasha Knight
Cover by Vanessa Hawthorne

First Samhain Publishing, Ltd. electronic publication: April 2007
First Samhain Publishing, Ltd. print publication: February 2008

Dedication

To Jessica, for hand holding.

To Mark for answering panicked emails.

To Sasha Knight for saying, "Add another 10k."

To Vanessa Hawthorne for being so patient with me about the cover.

And to Edwin. Never would have finished this without you... *huge hugs*

Prologue

He hadn't seen her in six years.

Zach winced. That wasn't exactly true. He had caught glimpses of her, laughing, chatting, but mainly leaving. Yes, mostly he had the memory of Anna Shrewsbury's back.

If he were sensible, that's the way he should leave it. Today, however, he didn't feel sensible. Anger knotted in his gut. He had just buried his partner and friend, Gregory Brabant, and he wasn't in the mood to be tolerant.

Zach scratched a hand through his hair and watched her take the hand of another concerned mourner; give the same weak, tired smile she had given to every other man.

The knot in his gut twisted tighter.

Had it become so practised now that it was second nature?

He knocked back his whiskey and was striding across the room before he realised. "Where's Sophia?"

Anna blinked, took a back step. Her hands tightened and her attention fixed on them. "She's resting. I think the strain of the day is too much for her."

Her voice was soft, shaky. Zach glared down at her but could only see golden strips of sunlight crossing her shining hair. He shoved his hand into his pocket. He would not touch her. His fingers curled tight. "So she left you here to sort everything."

"He was more than a brother-in-law to me, Zach."

Zach. His name on her lips stabbed an old pain through his chest. And that was just stupid. "Of course he was."

Her head snapped up. Her pale skin had flushed and fire sparked in her dark brown eyes. "He was." She stared around the room. Zach followed her gaze as it fell on the quietly murmuring mourners, most drinking one of Gregory's favourite malts. The cinema room was thick with people, interrupting the view of Gregory's beloved west garden. "I wanted to organise this wake. For...for him."

She swallowed and the shine of tears coated her eyes.

"You don't need to perform the act with me, Anna." He stared at his empty glass, wanting more so the sour burn could mask the fire already scorching his gut. "I've seen it too many times this morning. It's wearing thin."

"You're contemptible." Anna gripped the wet handkerchief in bloodless fingers. "If Gregory hadn't wanted you here, I'd throw you out, right now!"

"You do indignation so well."

"Just leave me alone, Zach."

"No." He snagged another glass from the long, white-clothed table behind Anna. "I think it's time I told you what I thought of you."

"This is hardly the time—"

"This is *exactly* the time."

He stared. She had just walked away, disappeared into the short stairwell that led up from the cinema room to the kitchen. Zach cursed under his breath and followed her.

"Anna." He twisted past the caterers, dumped his glass on a countertop and grabbed at her arm in the hallway. "Where the hell do you think you're going?"

"I am not having a fight with you in front of Gregory's friends." She wrenched her arm free.

"Then we'll have it here."

Her chin lifted. "If that's what you want."

Tension tightened his neck, his shoulders. What was he doing? He should leave her alone. He didn't need the scandal of being seen with a woman like her. But this was Anna, even when he hated her all he could see was the soft redness of her mouth. The remembered taste of her seared his tongue and the same old fire burned through his blood.

No. She would finally know what he thought of her. And then he would be finished with the damn woman.

"Here is just fine," he grated. He tugged the kitchen door shut. His gaze fixed on her. "You're a leech, Anna Shrewsbury."

She blinked and was silent.

"No denial? No little playacting to appeal to my better side?"

"You don't have a better side." She turned away from him again. "And if that's all you have to say—"

"No. It isn't." He caught her, pinned her against the wall. That soft red mouth trembled and he was so close to covering it with his own. The press of his hips into hers almost made him groan. "I want..." He couldn't speak.

"What, Zach?" Her dark eyes held his and he could see the need there. Her body was supple, pliant. Her hips moved, shifted tantalisingly against his. He groaned. "But can you afford me?"

The words soured his desire and familiar hatred replaced it. "It always comes down to the money with you." He stood back

9

from her and had the sudden urge to scrub away her touch. Her scent filled him.

"Yes, it does, doesn't it?" Anna's smile was sharp. "But then you don't expect anything else." She brushed a hand over the rumpled front of her black shift dress. "I think it *would* be better if you leave now. You've paid your respects." Her fingers had found her handkerchief again and started to fold and refold it. "Thank you for coming."

"So you are throwing me out."

Her dark gaze narrowed on him. "I'm amazed you made it here at all, Zach. That precious business even kept you from his deathbed."

Zach flinched. "I didn't—"

"Whatever." Anna looked grey, tired, and Zach had a twinge of unexpected guilt. Damn it, the woman made him insane. "Just go, Zach." She disappeared back into the kitchen. "I avoid you for a reason."

He just caught her fading words.

There was that tightening in his chest again.

Zach ignored it.

Chapter One

Anna tugged at her skirt.

Too short. Why had she believed Sofia when she said the beautifully tailored, but very *short* suit looked good on her? It was also a deep and burning red. Well, at least it matched her face. A grimace cut her mouth. Why did she listen to her sister, at all?

The lift pinged.

Anna straightened, resisting the last pull at the hem that ended too many inches above her knee. Mirrored steel doors slid back with a soft whoosh. Pale carpet stretched out before her and into a maze of steel and glass offices. The scent of polish. People hurrying past, the air thick with their voices.

The heels of her long boots sank into the deep carpet. Another of Sofia's suggestions. Why *did* she listen to her sister's fashion advice?

Because Sofia would make her life hell if she didn't.

Anna blew out a long, slow breath. "This is it." She willed herself to be calm, but her heart thudded.

Just a meeting with Gregory's solicitor. That's all it was. Her skin felt hot, flushed. She didn't have to be this nervous. She didn't.

Her nails cut into her palms.

It was just so hard to believe he was gone.

"Ah, Ms. Shrewsbury."

Anna bit at her lip, looked up and made herself smile. "Mr. Petersen."

She held out her hand and lost it to the old man's warm, heavy grip. His sharp eyes fixed on her. "I missed you at the funeral. I just want to say how sorry I am. How sorry we all are. Gregory Brabant was a good friend."

Her smile felt fake. "Thank you."

"Now, if you could just head to my office." He pointed down the long, glass-lined corridor. He smiled, something warm and reassuring. Yet Anna found she couldn't breathe any easier. This was too important to her. "I just have to get a few more things together."

"All right."

Anna watched him stride away. She fought the urge to scrub at her face as she turned down the corridor. Gregory had promised her. He said he had changed his will. That the house and the surrounding land would be hers. That Sofia would get none of it.

It had been their secret, hers and Gregory's. Every penny Anna had ever earned she had offered to him. But then he got sick and she had dropped the subject. Gregory was the one to bring it up again. He knew he was dying.

"Just go straight in."

Anna nodded her thanks to the Senior Partner's PA.

Her hand closed around the cold, steel handle. Yes. Sit in Carl Petersen's office. Stare out to the wide, plant-thick balcony overlooking the river and try just to breathe in and out. Find her calm place.

Gregory had promised.

And he had always been a man of his word.

Anna just wished the cold knot of dread in her stomach wasn't there.

Carl Petersen's office was much as she remembered it. Clean, clinical. Sunlight filtered through the wide, floor-to-ceiling windows, the shifting shadows of his numerous plants casting intricate patterns. The long blinds were closed on the inner, glass wall, blocking the stares of the staff.

For that, Anna was grateful.

She sank into one of the chairs set before his wide, neatly arranged desk. The soft scent of flowers drifted in. Anna breathed deep. Her heart started to patter and a shiver ran over her skin. What was he growing out there? It was...intoxicating.

Smiling to herself, she pulled at the hem of her skirt. It was worse now that she was sitting down. Far too much thigh. Yes. She could imagine one man's reaction to how she was dressed.

No. *He* would not invade her thoughts that day.

There were more important things to consider than a certain Zachary Quinn.

Her fingers ran along the hem of her skirt, nails skimming the soft fabric. She stared at her whitening knuckles and realised that her heart was thudding. Slow breaths. Slow. It was ridiculous that their brief exchange, a few words, should have her so rattled.

But then it wasn't just his words.

"Anna..."

Her heart jumped. Those measured tones, the subtle hint of disapproval. Hearing him as clearly as if he were right there.

"...Shrewsbury."

Her head snapped up.

Damn.

More than damn.

Anna's face flushed red raw, the heat of it scorching her skin. She knew she should speak, say something, anything, but her tongue was stuck to the roof of her mouth. Dry. Useless. And all she could do was stare.

Zachary Quinn.

He was there, standing in the open doorway to Carl Petersen's terrace.

Sunlight cast him in thick shadow, but the tall, straight frame was unmistakeable. At least to her. She had been avoiding it for six years. Light flickered a false halo of gold around his dark hair and she watched the familiar smoothing down of his jacket, his tie. Quiet. Calm. Collected. She hated that about him.

It forced words. "What are you doing here?" She heard the slow exhalation of his breath. And in his shadowed face, she made out the beginnings of a sharp grin. Her gut tightened. "Well?"

"Just as polite and well-mannered as I have come to expect."

"For you? Always."

The grin curled and Anna stopped her hands from fidgeting. Why was he here? "Did Carl Petersen double book?"

"So it would seem. Well..."

He moved.

Anna scrambled out of her chair.

Her plan for six long years jumped into action. Avoid. And if she couldn't do that, maintain distance. Always.

Steel blue eyes narrowed on her. His mouth flattened. "I was invited here, Anna."

No. That had to be wrong. "I'm here for the reading of Gregory's will. Mr. Petersen said—"

Zach drew closer.

Anna found herself gripping the back of the chair, fingertips digging into the cool leather. He was out of the shadows now, sunlight cutting across his profile. Her heart missed a beat. She hated him. She did. But that couldn't stop her from knowing, *knowing* how beautiful he was.

She stomped on those thoughts and made herself hold his hard gaze.

"Are you trying to defend yourself, Anna?"

His attention fixed on her clenching hands and his smile deepened. His gaze lifted. A glimmer of wry humour shone there. "Hardly necessary, I assure you. I can *contain* myself."

Anger twisted a knot tight, aching in her gut. Overreacting. He always made her feel as if she was overreacting to him, making her feel stupid. She straightened and pulled her hands away from the comfort of the chair. She lifted her chin. Fine. He'd been invited. She could sit with the man for the short time it took to read the rest of Gregory's will. Couldn't she?

But surely, Carl would have told her about Zach? Anna wet her lips. "Why...?"

A spike of silver shone in his eyes. They narrowed. Firm lips curved and Anna found herself staring, staring...

"...can I contain myself?" Zach's voice was like a slow run of honey over her heated skin.

Anna blinked. It was suddenly hard to breathe, her chest tight, trapped. She had to get away. Had to.

"You shouldn't ask me questions like that, Anna."

She shook her head, trying to force some sense back. This was Zach. He enjoyed playing games like this. A game. Always a game. That reminder made a smile cut her mouth. "Why did he invite you, Zach? That was my question." She saw a carafe of water on a side table. Good. An excuse to move further away. And it would not look like running. Which it wasn't. "Anything else is just in your mind."

She closed her fingers tight around the handle and willed her arm not to shake. Cool water splashed into a crystal tumbler. With the glass in her hand, she turned back to him. Zach hadn't moved. "Well?"

"I'm a beneficiary."

Anna blinked. "I thought everything had been sorted last week? That this was an oversight?"

There was his patronising smile that he saved just for her. Her fingers crushed around the glass. "No. It seems"—he glanced to the neatly stacked papers on Carl Peterson's desk— "that Gregory set these particular bequests aside as a stipulation in the will."

"You snooped through Carl's papers?"

"You'd like to think that of me, wouldn't you?"

Anna had never met a man she'd wanted to slap more. "Fine." She bit out the word. "The sooner this is over with the better."

"Yes."

A slowly drawn-out word and she found Zach's attention sliding over what she was wearing. Heat burned in her face. Again. Only he ever looked at her that way, appraising but...irritated. She would never be good enough. Anna cut out those thoughts too. Whether Zach found her even remotely attractive was completely unimportant.

"Have you finished?"

"I am always *impressed* by your fashion sense."

"What I wear has nothing to do with you."

His smile made her grit her teeth. He delayed on the length of exposed thigh. "Obviously not."

She would not give him the satisfaction of getting angry. Anna willed herself to breathe. Slow. Even breaths. She focused on the clear water in her glass. Watched the light reflect, refract.

"That skirt should only have a private audience."

Anna felt the blush to the roots of her hair. Damn Sofia. But she would never admit to *him* that she hadn't chosen these clothes. That she wasn't perfectly confident, comfortable in them.

"Surely, you must be used to these comments, Anna."

She glared at him. The smug, sanctimonious— "What I wear has nothing to do with anyone else. It doesn't suggest anything, invite anything."

His features hardened. "You knew I'd be here."

Anna bit down on a curse. Everything always revolved around him. Always had. Always would. "D'you really think I'd be standing in this office if I knew *you* would be here?" A bitter laugh escaped her. "I do my very best to avoid you, Zach. That must be obvious. Even to you."

"Really?"

She would not rise to that bait.

Instead, she escaped to the balcony. Get away from him. That was always the safer option, because sometimes... Anna could still feel the heat in her cheeks. Sometimes she would begin to fall into the intense blue of his eyes. And then her body, her senses, would start to remember.

Anna cursed under her breath and knocked back her glass of water. Tepid. She grimaced.

A river breeze lifted her short, bobbed hair, washed some of the heat from her blood. She put her empty glass on the edge of the stone planter. Her fingertips caressed the narrow leaves, the velvet soft petals of the bush dappled with sunlight. Better to touch that, than think about running them over the thick darkness of a certain man's hair.

"Blushing Bride." His voice, too close behind her.

Anna closed her eyes and stopped herself from sighing. Couldn't the man take a hint? "I know. Gregory has a border of them." She didn't look at him. "I came out here to carry on avoiding you."

"I could start to take this personally, Anna." There was laughter in that smooth voice.

He thought this was *funny*?

She turned. Despite her heels adding inches to her tall height, she only found her gaze level with his mouth and met the familiar hard plane of his jaw. It would be sleek and warm to her touch. She clung to the ball of anger burning in her gut. "I wish you would." Strong, confident. Good.

His mouth twitched, compressed into a thin line.

Anna was aware of every breath that expanded, contracted her lungs. And with it, she tried not to breathe in his clean, male scent, spiced with a hint of something that had her pulse throbbing. She never let herself get this close to him.

It was a mistake.

It was *always* a mistake.

She had to escape.

His hand closed around her upper arm.

The jolt of his touch, even through layers of clothes, startled her. They couldn't touch. They mustn't.

"Let go of me, Zach."

His fingers dropped away. "At the funeral. You took offence. I'm sorry..."

Anna blinked. Zachary Quinn. Apologising? It was unheard of.

"...but what I said was true."

She gripped the anger tight to her. Felt it flare and burn bright. Wanted her glare to scorch him. "You accused me of living off Gregory like a leech."

"Well. Haven't you?" He caught the hand that flew to his jaw. "I had to watch a man I loved and respected make a fool of himself over your sister. Worse. Marry her," he grated.

She wrenched her hand free. "And whose fault was that?"

He blinked.

"Whose *wife* introduced Sofia to him?"

"*Ex*-wife." Zach's face froze into a hard line. "We are not discussing Isabelle."

"When do you ever?" She let out a slow breath. "Gregory loved Sofia. And she loved Gregory."

"More fool him. And more fool you for thinking Sofia loves anyone but herself."

Nothing he said would hurt her anymore. Nothing. "You're just worried about the business. That's all."

"Yes." His eyes drilled her. "Sofia splashes out money like water. I made sure that she wouldn't get any more of it."

"What?"

"Ah-h." A cruel smile cut his mouth. "Now you start to worry. Gregory came to his senses before the end. He chopped Sofia out of the business. Surely, she told you what he left her in his will?"

Anna blinked. She hadn't asked. She had just assumed everything related to business had passed onto Sofia as Gregory's wife. That included the massive corporation that had made Gregory and Zach so incredibly wealthy. She had no interest in it. She just wanted the land and the house that had belonged to her family.

And the freedom it promised.

"I didn't ask."

Zach laughed. "Anna Shrewsbury not worrying when her next fat cheque would arrive? Hardly likely."

She would not try to justify her life to him. Let him think what he liked. He saw her as a money-grabbing harridan. Fine. She wouldn't let something as obscuring as the truth cloud him. She never had.

Anna looked up from the exotic palm sweeping its leaves over the edge of the terrace wall. "What upsets you most, Zach?" Fury burned in her gut. Oh, yes. She had her own arsenal. "That I happily lived off Gregory? Or that *you* couldn't buy me?"

She saw a muscle jump in his cheek.

Good. She had broken through his icy control. See how he liked to be insulted.

Anna stalked towards him, her gaze never leaving his, seeing the spark of his anger. The sensible part of her mind screamed at her not to bait this man. But she ignored it. Damn him. And she could damn herself right along with him.

"Because you did think about it, Zach. Once. Six years ago."

"I don't buy women."

His voice was strained, thick with anger. She could see his irritation in his tight jaw, the narrowing of his eyes.

"You offered..." Anna was determined to play the vamp he thought she was. He had no idea how far that was from reality. But then, Zach didn't care about the truth. "I was only nineteen." She made a smile curve her mouth and she looked at him from under her lashes. "How was I to know that you were so *very* wealthy?"

"Stop this, Anna."

"But then being in Gregory Brabant's circle, I met so *many* men."

"I said—"

"Ones who offered—"

"No."

The word was a quiet growl. His fingers slid around her neck, her jaw, his thumb pressed against her cheek.

Contact stopped her words.

Hot skin touching hers, the slight rasp of calluses. Her heart skittered. They couldn't touch. They just couldn't.

He stroked her, a soft caress slipping over her cheek, edging closer. It was hard to breathe. His thumb caught her lip and she gasped.

Zach smiled and his eyes gleamed. "You melt when I touch you."

His voice eased over her, the deep pulse of sound finding the throb low, low in her belly. His thumb slowly traced over her burning mouth. Oh God... She should stop this. She had to stop this.

His breath brushed her ear. "You always have."

"No."

"So you don't want me to touch you?"

"I—"

"Here?"

His mouth moved in a brief warm brush over her forehead.

"Here?"

Her eyelid, the spikes of her lashes fluttering against his lips.

"Here?"

So close to her mouth, she could almost taste him. The teasing had fire in her blood. He did this to her. Teased. Played.

Well, no more.

She took his mouth.

His shock lasted a heartbeat.

They stumbled back, Zach hitting the solid, glass wall of the terrace with a low groan. Half lying against him, her fingers tight in his hair, her other hand worming beneath his jacket, Anna nibbled, tasted, her tongue finding his.

All thought but him had gone.

And his hands, sliding down her body, hitching at her mercifully short skirt. Finding her.

Anna moaned into his mouth.

Zach had burned in her blood for six long years. Finally to have him.

"You're a piece of work, Anna." The words were growled in anger against her lips.

For a moment, she froze and something inside her cracked.

Zach had been playing her. Again. And she'd flung herself at him with complete and idiotic abandon. Horror crawled up her spine.

Anna scrambled out of his loose hold, desperate to straighten her skirt, blouse, jacket. She ran trembling fingers through her tangled hair, but couldn't look him in the eye.

Zach's laugh was bitter. "So you find out that Sofia has lost her forty percent share in the business. Your sister won't be able to afford her lifestyle. And yours. So what do you do?"

Stung, Anna glared at him. "You started this."

He brushed the front of his expensive jacket smooth, fixed his tie. "Did I?" Zach's attention travelled over her still rumpled suit. "Sofia put you up to it."

"How dare you!"

Anna had to get away from him. Far away. Starting with this bloody terrace. After this meeting, if she never saw him again it would be too soon.

Zach grabbed her arm. "Don't play games with me, Anna." His voice was a harsh whisper. "Because I play them well. Too well."

She tugged herself free. "Oh, I know that."

The low creak of the outer door. Anna's attention shot to it. Damn. Carl Petersen was back. Heat still scorched her skin. Her lips were swollen and any trace of lipstick would be long gone. She refused to look at Zach to see if it was smeared over his mouth.

"My pride and joy," Carl Petersen declared, smiling, his arms full of papers. "Better than sitting in this stuffy office, but..." He looked at his loaded arms. "The winds would blow all this into the river. Come. Sit down."

He groaned and dropped his papers carefully onto the desk, arranging them neatly. "Would you like tea, coffee?"

"I think we'd both like tea, thank you," Zach murmured, holding out Anna's chair for her to sit.

She sat, fighting the need to stick her very sharp boot heel into his toe. She took an even breath. "Yes. Thank you." She gave Carl a quick smile, watching him as he chatted on the intercom with his PA. Her fingers started to play with the hem of her skirt.

A prickle ran over her skin and Anna could feel Zach's gaze burning into her thigh.

She would not look. She would *not* look.

Gleaming eyes held her. An eyebrow lifted.

"So."

Anna shot her attention back to the solicitor, her face red. She hated Zach.

One of the most important days of her life, one of the most vital...and Zach had her mind in pieces.

"You know why you're here." Carl slit open a large, white envelope with a slim knife. "Gregory Brabant, in his wisdom, decided that he wanted to divide his will. Sofia's bequest was read last week, along with the minor beneficiaries. Yours..." he pulled out the document with a sigh, "...is a *little* more complicated."

Sudden tension had her neck knotted.

Gregory had promised her. He said the land that had belonged to her family for generations, that the house her mother had restored would be hers. Sofia wanted to sell them both. A developer was offering a high price...but Gregory had been holding out. He knew, *knew* that it was the only thing that could connect her to her parents. Anna closed her eyes. He had promised.

"...and now to the meat of it."

Damn. She had to listen.

"These are Gregory Brabant's own words. He stated that you must not comment, nor interrupt." Carl looked over his glasses, his pale eyes sharp. "No matter how much you may need to."

Anna stopped the need to fidget. What had Gregory done?

"'People have often complained about my sense of humour. Tough.'" The solicitor shifted uneasily in his seat and his attention remained fixed on the documents in his hands. "'No doubt both of you will curse me. But that's tough too.'"

Despite her nerves that had a run of sweat trickling down the back of her neck, Anna had to smile. Her heart tightened. She would miss Gregory.

"'Zach, you've been like a son to me. Your own father couldn't have been more proud. And so to you I leave Middleton Cottage and its ten acres.'"

Anna gasped, her hand flying to her mouth to stop herself from crying out. He had given *her* house, *her* land to Zach. What was Gregory thinking?

"Please, Ms. Shrewsbury." Carl kept his voice low. "Nothing until I have read it through."

She jerked a nod, but could feel the start of tears. The only happy times remembered in her life were in that house. And it had all ended when she was nine. Now Zach had the only thing she wanted in the world.

Zach bristled, no doubt seething with angered questions. Anna ignored him.

"'Anna...'"

Her attention shot to the will.

"'You listened, you laughed, you were with *me*. And so I leave to you my forty percent share of Quinn Brabant Technologies.'"

"No."

"Anna." Zach's voice, calm, controlled but she could hear the throb of fury. "Let him finish."

"Thank you," Carl said.

His neck was flushed red and his nerves were also starting to mottle his jaw. Anna suddenly felt sorry for the man. The one thing that had always annoyed her about Gregory was his love of practical jokes. She'd never stood for them. Had told him that. Many times. Now her brother-in-law was having the last laugh on her.

"'Shame I can't be here to see your faces, but that's the nature of a will, isn't it? You both want what the other has. So I have a deal for you.

"'One week. You last together one week. Twenty-four hours a day for seven days.

"'You refuse to do this? You don't last the week? And everything goes to Sofia. Everything.

"'And it starts from…now.'"

Chapter Two

Anna couldn't look at Zach.

Carl Petersen put the will down, took off his glasses and scrubbed his hands over his face. "I'm sorry. I tried to talk him out of this childishness. But he was adamant."

A knock on the door made Anna jump. Smiling, his PA brought in a tray and placed it on the desk. The woman poured tea Anna didn't drink. She held the delicate cup and saucer out of habit.

And she still couldn't look at Zach.

Gregory had always known that they hadn't gotten on. However, he had never known the reason. A week with Zach. For years, *years* she had avoided him, managing only minutes in his company. Her insides tightened into an aching knot. Gregory had probably imagined rows and sulky silences, all of which would have amused him no end.

Not...

No her mind wasn't going there.

"And he was in full charge of all his capacities?"

Zach's unruffled voice broke into her panic. How could he be so damned calm? Millions and millions of pounds of something he thought was his had just been given to his worst nightmare. Her.

"Yes," Anna said, before the solicitor could. Her voice was tight. "I was with him at...at the end. He was perfectly lucid."

Steel blue eyes speared her. Cold. Narrowed. "Yes." He looked back to Carl. "Was it confirmed?"

The solicitor tapped the document on his desk. "Because of this, I made absolutely certain." He glanced at Anna. "It's only a week."

"Sofia has agreed to this?"

Carl sat back in his chair. "Gregory discussed it with her. Apparently, he had her full support."

Zach muttered something Anna couldn't catch. She stared at him, watched his hand rub over his jaw, his attention fixed on the scattered documents on the desk. They had no choice. And somewhere Gregory was laughing himself silly.

"One week?" Zach asked.

Anna closed her eyes. She put the cooling tea back onto the tray. Something she wouldn't put a name to rushed through her. She didn't need this.

She stared at her hands, at the tight knuckles.

Sofia had known.

Had *dressed* her.

Anna felt the blood rise under her skin again. Her sister had probably amused herself with provoking the very correct, very disapproving Zachary Quinn. Would be laughing about it with her cronies at that very minute.

But the damn man was right about one thing. Sofia had a lifestyle to maintain. Gregory must have left her everything else. Had to. The houses, the other businesses not under Zach's control.

God...she was so stupid not to talk about the will with her sister.

"So you agree?" Anna made herself say the words and found both men staring at her. "Agree to Gregory's silly plan? This time next week, what we want is ours."

"No," Zach said. He stared at Carl. "There has to be a way out of this."

"Are you refusing to agree to the terms?" the solicitor asked.

"No. He isn't."

Zach glared at her. "I am perfectly capable—"

"Fine," Anna said. "Argue, but refuse and everything goes to Sofia. I want my house and my land, Zach. And if that means a week with you? Then so be it."

He let out a slow breath. "This is insane. It isn't legal."

"Gregory has set his terms. Sofia hasn't contested. Nothing in your partnership agreement can undo it."

Carl pushed back his chair and stood. "I'll leave you for a few moments to discuss it. If you agree, then I will give you the full details." He sighed. "Not before." His glance flicked over both of them. "Again, I'm sorry."

Anna's mouth opened. Leave? He couldn't leave her alone with Zach.

And then the enormity of what was ahead of her crashed through. Seven days and nights, *nights* alone with Zach. "I can't do this."

Zach stood, refastening the buttons on his jacket. "Now who's refusing?"

"This wasn't my idea." She wiped her hand over her face. "As if I wanted, needed this."

"Yes." He stared out to the terrace. "It's all very convenient for you, isn't it?" He glared at her. "Sofia told you."

What? "No."

"You have no intention of doing this. Your sister gets everything. And you get what?" His narrowed gaze pierced her. "Yes." The suppressed fury made her shiver. "You're going to carve it up between you."

Anna pushed herself to her feet, feeling the flare of hot anger rise with her. "I knew nothing about this." Her spine locked, hands tightening into fists at her side. Zach had his very fixed image of her. She'd deliberately helped him form it. "I wanted *my* house. I couldn't care less about your bloody company."

A cutting smile. "Not care about the wealth that owning even a fraction of it would bring? I doubt it." He laughed . "I know you, Anna." His gaze dropped to her mouth and her heart clenched. She couldn't breathe. "Intimately."

The dark promise in his voice turned her legs to water.

Damn him. A look, a word and she was jelly. No. She wasn't a young girl anymore, overawed by the presence of infamous Zachary Quinn. She wasn't.

Anna matched that smile. "Not as intimately as you would've liked."

A muscle jumped in his cheek.

Her smile grew, but the victory tasted strangely bitter. "In fact, hardly at all." But why could she only focus on his mouth, his lips, the remembered taste of him still there on her tongue? And the need for her fingers to brush over the warmth of his skin, slip—

Angry with herself, she glared at him and pulled in a tight breath. "So we tell Carl that we agree."

"There will be rules." Zach turned away, began to pace a short stretch of carpet, ignoring her. Anna gritted her teeth. The man was infuriating.

"Rules?"

"Gregory and his sense of humour."

He muttered a foul curse under his breath. Anna blinked. Zach? Swearing? The man who, when she was fifteen, had strong words with her Head Teacher when she used the word damn?

More fierce strides covered the carpet and Zach stared up at the ceiling. "I hope you're finding this funny, old man." He blew out a hot breath, stopped pacing and focused on her. "Yes. Rules. I won't put my life on hold. And I will *not* enter any place that has Sofia Brabant in it."

Everything was always about him.

Anna felt a smile pull at her mouth. Well, if he wanted his company... "I have a show tonight. Sofia is the principal patron."

She let those words sink in, watched his face darken and the anger clench his jaw. Her own gut was tight. It was the artist's first big show. Sofia's new fad was her being seen fostering new, bright talent. Freddie Lewis was brilliant. Anna wanted it to go well for him. She'd worked hard to get the right people to see his work. It was the least she could do, after the trouble she had caused him.

No. Not thinking about that.

And it was what she did, made all of Sofia's grand gestures a reality. Until her sister got bored.

Anna squashed down the sour burn.

With Gregory's promise, she thought she'd have a chance to escape her sister. But he'd made it worse. Zach would find a way out, or tie the will up for months. Years? Her smile faded.

Her dream of escape was falling to ashes.

"Damn it, Zach, we can be adults about this." She looked back to the desk and the piles of paper. An envelope with her name? Her heart jumped. She'd recognise Gregory's spidery script anywhere. "Play the game for one week."

"And will you?"

Anna pulled her attention away from the mysterious envelope. "I have to."

He gave her that slow smile, which sent a shiver over her skin. She ignored it. "Play adult games?"

Anna cursed the hot flush burning her face. "You know I didn't mean it like that."

His grin grew, something wicked, predatory. He moved closer and Anna willed her feet to stay planted. And not run. Fast. Far. "I've always enjoyed your gauche act, Anna."

His scent filled her, making breathing hard, making her blood pound.

A fingertip traced a slow run over her flushed cheek, her skin tingling in its wake.

"And we both know that it *is* an act."

The old pain crushed her heart. Protection. From him. Zach *consumed* women. Was infamous for it. But only a certain type of woman appealed to him. Someone pure, innocent. Corruptible. She knew this from personal experience. And Anna had made certain that he believed the opposite of her.

"Yes." She made the seductive smile curve her mouth. If she played this game with him, she was safe. Her stupid heart could never fall for a man like him. She had to tell herself that. Over. And over. "I know my *charm* wore thin for you."

His eyes narrowed and a spike of silver gleamed there. "We could always pretend that you never betrayed me."

The cold words jolted Anna out of her game. Betrayed? Yes. Her nails dug sharp in her palms. Yes. She had, hadn't she?

"So, have you decided?" Carl Petersen bustled back into the room.

"It will be...interesting," Zach murmured.

The solicitor dropped into his chair and hunted through his papers. "That's a yes from both of you?"

Anna found herself under Carl's scrutiny. She jerked a nod.

He had agreed. She could still feel his cold glare boring into her. In that second, she wished he hadn't.

"Then here's the rest of it." Carl pushed his glasses further up his long nose and flipped through more documents. "He has some rules you both must follow."

Anna glanced involuntarily at Zach, but found only his hard profile.

"Firstly." Carl looked up, focused on Zach. "Ms. Shrewsbury must move into your city apartment."

Anna closed her eyes. Damn Gregory Brabant for thinking this was funny. She'd not set foot there. Not since *that* night.

Zach must have nodded because the solicitor moved on.

"The...the sleeping arrangements..." Carl reddened and then he rushed, "...are to be at your own discretion."

Zach muttered a string of curses. Anna concentrated on breathing in and out, and trying not to see Carl's bright red face. Gregory had never known what had fuelled their antipathy. She could never tell him.

"Second. This is your secret—"

"But Sofia knows—" Anna broke in.

To tell no one. Her stomach clenched. They would look like a...couple. No. They could be discreet.

Carl shook his head. "Gregory has ensured her silence."

Zach's soft chuckle startled Anna. "Now her compliance makes sense. He threatened to cut her off completely. Didn't he?"

"That is a private matter for Mrs. Brabant—"

"That's a yes, then."

"And finally," Carl broke in. "This must be played out in public."

Anna stopped herself from groaning. She hated the glare of attention Gregory's wealth had commanded. Add Zach's media profile and his notorious obsession with privacy... It really was going to be hell.

Zach snapped out of his chair. "She moves in. We look very public. No one knows it's a Brabant practical joke. Does that sum it up?"

"Mr. Quinn..."

"Yes or no?"

Zach held his gaze until the older man sighed. "Yes."

"I saw a letter..." Anna half gestured to the stacks of papers crowding his desk. "And what is all that?"

Carl Petersen's mouth gave a wry twist. "I'm trying to keep all of Gregory's bequests together. It's the most convoluted..." He straightened. "The letter is for this time, a week from today. There's one for both of you."

Zach glanced at his watch. "I'm already late." His gaze slid over her and his mouth compressed. "You'll have to do."

The familiar jolt of anger gripped her. "Do?"

"I will see you again in a week," Carl said. The older man stood and moved out from behind his desk. Anna found him holding her hand. The concern softening his face made her bite at her lip. "Good luck," he murmured. "I wish Gregory hadn't put you in this position."

Anna did too. But then she did what she did best; she put on the mask, made herself smile. "I could hardly deny Gregory his last laugh."

"No. Indeed." He shook Zach's hand, short, hard. "Until next week."

Zach opened the door, let her precede him.

His voice was no more than a whisper. "He's worried about you."

Anna tried to ignore the brush of his breath over her ear, her temple. Tried and failed. She walked faster.

Zach matched her pace easily. "And he has a right to be."

"I'm not listening to your threats, Zach."

Her finger stabbed at the lift button and she stared up at the floor indicator. Get back to her room, throw stuff in a case. Get out before she had to face Sofia. Her sister was out at lunch and that lasted hours. Anna cringed away from what Sofia would say.

"Not threats. A promise."

"Zach..."

The lift pinged.

She rushed forward.

Anna watched the doors close, catching her distorted reflection in the mirrored steel. And Zach, leaning again the metal rail. Calm. Relaxed. But his gaze drilled her. She had to look away and inwardly groaned. The skirt really was minute.

With a judder, the lift started to descend.

"You will behave yourself this week, Anna."

Her eyes clashed with his in the mirrored doors. "I'm not twelve."

"No."

His stare slid all too slowly down her body. Awareness prickled over her skin and she fought down the rush in her blood. Anger. It was anger. How dare he look—

"I've watched you wage war with this body."

The murmur of his words licked over her skin. The power that simply his voice could command was embarrassing. No, it wasn't anger, but something much more destructive. Anna shut her eyes, desperate to deny it, and caught his scent, breathed him in. Deep. Her heart skittered.

The brush of his suit as he moved around her, the soft rhythm of his breathing, flickered fire over her skin, skin sensitive to his slightest stir. Totally, achingly aware of him.

This was why she was never alone with Zach.

He wove his charm, caught her, spun her mind with needs and stupid wants.

He leaned in close. "Conquering idiotic, weak-willed men."

Yes. He teased her. Enjoyed it. She could hear the satisfied smile in his voice.

His finger traced the outer edge of her lip and she gasped. Her eyes shot open, met Zach's darkened gaze. Her mouth was dry. And she ached to taste him.

"But not this week, Anna. This week, you're mine. Do you understand?"

His.

Blood pounded.

But then sense pulled her back.

She would never be his toy. Something to be played with and put back on the shelf when he was bored. After last time, did he think she was completely stupid? "I don't belong to you." She stepped back, found her spine up against the cold steel of the rail. "This is Gregory's last joke." A sharp smile twisted her mouth. "And you have more to lose. My sister will own a huge chunk of your precious company."

Something changed in his face. It settled into hard, pitiless lines, his jaw tight.

"Don't threaten me, Anna." Her heart missed a beat at the sudden cold spike to his voice. "You will see out this week. You will behave as I pay my women to behave."

Heat bled into her face and her insides shrivelled.

"I am *not* your woman."

One of the silent, perfect women photographed on his arm. Dutiful. Empty. Yes. His admission was a slip. However much he denied it, money always formed the basis of his dealings with women.

"No. You're not." His attention shifted to her mouth. "Not yet."

Damn the man. She willed her voice to be strong. "Not ever, Zach."

"So your game plan has changed?"

He gripped the rail, blocking her with his body. He was too close. Anna focused on the knot of his tie, letting her gaze sink into the deep, dark red silk...because if she didn't... If she looked up—

No. She let out a controlled breath. "Sorry. You're confusing me with someone who finds you attractive."

The low rumble of his laughter surrounded her. Despite her best efforts, the edges of her mouth quirked up.

"Women have thrown themselves at me since I reached puberty, Anna. You..." his thumb lifted her chin, making her look at him, "...have proven to be no exception."

He was beautiful. Anna could never deny that. Something about him called to her, a dizzying rush of need making her forget almost everything else. But she had resisted and she would continue to resist.

Zach was cold, cruel, heartless.

She knew his ex-wife, Isabelle. Their divorce hadn't burned through the tabloids. Zach's lawyers must have seen to that. But Isabelle had dropped hints, too many to ignore. Then there was Anna's own, more personal experience.

"No." Anna ducked under his arm, escaped to another corner of the wide lift. She straightened her jacket. Stopped herself from tugging at her skirt. "This isn't the deal, Zach." She willed her heart into an even rhythm. "Before...in Carl's office." She felt herself flush and cursed silently. "I was stupid. *It* was stupid."

He stared at the floor indicator before focusing on her. "You know I can never trust you." His voice was matter-of-fact and something about that stung Anna. "Never will, again."

"Fine."

"But you will not humiliate me—"

"Your precious ego," Anna muttered. "Heaven forbid a woman should even *look* at anyone else—"

Zach punched the emergency stop.

The lift juddered.

"You did more than look, Anna."

"I—"

Fury burned through him. She could see it in the tightness of his jaw, the balled fists. And his eyes, sparking silver fire. His ice façade had fallen away...and for a brief, brief moment, she saw his passion, his power.

The drone of the emergency alarm warning faded.

Everything faded.

There was only the thrum of her blood.

Anna wanted him.

Now.

Chapter Three

"Oh no."

He took a back step. His eyes fixed on her. Wary. The show of anger slid from him, the icy mask falling into place. A hard smile tugged at his mouth. "You can't catch me twice with that."

Anna only then realised what she had wanted, what she had almost done. Heat slashed her face. She scrubbed at her eyes and she willed her heart to slow. Throwing herself at him. Again.

And Zach had rejected her.

That didn't matter. It didn't. She should see it as a blessing. He had stopped her from making another complete fool of herself. That feeling deep in her gut was relief. It was.

"As I was saying..."

He released the emergency stop and the lift groaned, then started to descend.

Anna focused her attention on the electronic floor numbers. His voice was infuriatingly calm. She really hated that about him.

"...you will act respectably in public." The lift pinged and the doors slid back. "I had to interrupt an important lunch for this"—his gaze speared her—"silliness."

Anna gritted her teeth, biting back the curses she wanted to hurl at him. A lunch? Damn. She would have to sit in a glass-boxed office and listen to senior executives drone on. And it wasn't as if she didn't have her own work to do. But at least lunch couldn't go on *all* afternoon.

"I know how to behave."

"Of course you do." Zach scanned the underground garage. "You had your sister as a fine example."

She ignored him. The air stank of car fumes and damp concrete. Somewhere in the lines of luxury cars was her battered little run around... Ah, there it was. "My car's that way—"

Zach gripped her elbow. "I'm sure it is. But mine is this way."

Anna pulled her arm free. "I can drive myself."

"I don't intend to lose sight of you for a minute." His fingers curled again around her elbow and propelled her forward. "That way you won't be able to report back to Petersen that I broke the deal."

"You keep forgetting that I'll lose too."

Zach's laugh was bitter. "Your sort never loses."

"My sort?" Anna stopped and picked his fingers away from her arm. "And what would that be, Zach?"

"I'm not having this argument here."

Her smile was sharp. "Then where?"

"Mr. Quinn, sir."

A blank-faced, uniformed chauffeur held open the door to a gleaming black Bentley.

"Inside."

Still seething, adrenalin making her blood rush, she climbed into the back of the car, trying to keep her skirt over her thighs. Pale leather seats didn't help. And she could feel Zach's eyes on her. What did he think she was going to do? Make a run for it? Flirt with the chauffeur?

The door shut with a soft clunk.

In the few seconds she was alone, Anna tugged at her skirt, wiggling. Damn Sofia for this. And damn herself for listening to her.

The other passenger door opened. Anna flushed and stopped twisting. Her hands rested over her knees. A futile gesture.

"Seat belt," Zach said.

Anna closed her eyes. She should've done that first...then wiggled. She let out a slow breath and pulled the belt across her chest. She would be calm. Rising to everything Zach said and did was getting her nowhere.

Calm.

She could do this.

It was just that she was a little out of practice. She had avoided him so successfully it had made her forget the effect he had on her.

The car softly rumbled into life and pulled out. Smooth, almost silent. The interior smelt of expensive leather and something else. Something that made her heart beat faster, made a pulse jump low, low in her pelvis.

Zach's scent.

No.

Calm.

Her finger traced absently over the pale skin of her knee, drawing out the old, faint scar. A legacy of an early childhood spent scrambling over walls, up trees. Of the only time she remembered being happy, of being truly loved.

Her jaw clenched.

If she stayed calm then the week wouldn't be so bad. At its end, she would have the house in which she grew up, a place connecting her to generations of her mother's family. For the first time in years, she would have a home.

And she could not, would not let her past with Zach deny her that.

Her attention slid to Zach, flicking over his stern profile. His jaw was tight and he seemed lost in his own thoughts. But she had to start to build up *civilised* behaviour between them. "Will there still be food?"

"I imagine." A sharp smile tugged at his mouth. "Though it's doubtful that you would eat any of it."

Anna remembered to be calm, remembered that she wasn't going to be stupid. She was going to be sensible. Not rise to his taunts.

Her fingers rubbed at her knee and she fixed her thoughts there. She needed a distraction. There'd always been the sly comments about how thin she was. No, she was not sinking to his level. "I live on more than lettuce, Zach." She toned down the edge to her smile, though her gut was tight. "Some days there's even dressing."

His lips twitched. "Careful now," he murmured. "I might start to think you've eaten a whole meal in the last month."

Anna bit back the words she wanted to lash at him.

There had been a gleam to his eyes. He *knew* she was trying to stay polite. And he was deliberately goading her. No. Calm. She was calm. He could be childish if he wanted—

The smile on his mouth widened.

And that need to slap him shot back.

"Don't even think it, Anna."

"What?"

He leaned in close and Anna forced herself not to shrink away. The warmth of his breath stirred her skin. She bit her lip. His mouth, so close, almost touching...

"Misbehave. I dare you." The softly spoken words sent a shiver deep through her body. "And it will give me the very good excuse to put you over my knee and spank you."

His words infused her with a promise of pleasure...and her stupid, stupid imagination ran with so much more. Anna could feel his lips curve into a smile over the sensitive shell of her ear. She remembered the heat of his mouth, the taste of him, large hands moulding—

Her fingers gripped her knees to stop their trembling.

This was insane.

"Misbehave, Anna." A ripple of quiet laughter had her nails digging deep. "I *double* dare you."

This was why she hated him.

He could reduce her to a shuddering wreck in moments and to him it was all a game. Not that she *could* care for a man like Zach. No. A quivering mess she might be, but she was not completely stupid.

Anna took a steadying breath. "You don't want to start this, Zach."

"Why?"

That one little word tempted her. To lose herself and the week in him.

And then reality crashed into her daydream.

It would all have to come out, the lies that had twisted the last six years. No. She didn't do relationships. And seven days was a relationship to her. Had been since that short, disastrous engagement to Freddie Lewis.

Thoughts of Freddie made her cringe.

Zach stilled.

"You're right." His voice was cold, clipped.

He sat back and chill air replaced the warmth of his breath, the brush of his lips. Sensible. It was sensible. Teenage hormones couldn't influence her now. But she couldn't look at him.

Zach knew how attractive he was to women. How he could turn them to mush with a single glance, a few whispered words.

It was obvious. Even with her, a woman he hated, that it was a game he couldn't stop himself playing.

Anna made herself look out of the window. She blinked. She knew the way to his central office. This wasn't it.

"Where are we going?"

"To lunch."

"Lunch? But I thought..."

His smile was cutting. "...that you could enjoy watching my befuddled senior executives simper over you?" The Bentley turned onto a side road and stopped before the entrance to a luxurious hotel. The chauffeur climbed out.

Anna let the seat belt slide back into place. This was why Zach had frowned at her choice of clothes. She could feel the heat already staining her cheeks.

The chauffeur opened the passenger door and she murmured her thanks. Anna swung her legs out and tried not to let the general public see any more of her thighs. It would be laughable. It would. If she wasn't so mortified.

"Shall we?" Zach offered his arm.

Anna's fingers curled into his arm, pressing the soft, cool material of his sleeve. Up the steps to the dark wooded revolving door. Anna pushed her way inside, caught the narrowed eye of the smartly dressed man behind the wide curve of the desk...until he found Zach following after her.

The man's expression slid into a well-rehearsed simper.

"Welcome, Mr. Quinn." He waved a finger at a porter. "Please show—"

"That's all right, thank you, Edward. I know the way."

His arm was on offer again.

Fine. A formal lunch. Sharing a meal with a few of the very senior executives. She may have even met them before, so the awkward explaining of who she was exactly would be easier. She would sit, have incredible food, they would talk figures and acronyms about which she'd know nothing. It would be an almost pleasant afternoon...

A man in a smart black uniform, smiling, opened a door.

...or not.

Every head turned.

There had to be fifty, sixty of them at least, crowding the sumptuous and ornately gilded room. In reflex, her fingers dug into Zach's arm. She could feel her cheeks burning.

"My father's memorial lunch."

Anna's stomach hit her feet. Gregory's will had dragged Zach away from this. "I...I didn't know."

"Really?" His voice was sharp. "I thought you dressed for the occasion."

Damn it. It looked that way.

Had Gregory's will also held a stipulation on when it should be read? He *had* wanted them to be public. And parading them in front of all of the company's senior people, Zach's family and friends...

Had Sofia realised?

She'd tutted over Anna's conservative and staid wardrobe. Said she had something in her own vast collection of clothes that was a little too big on her.

Damn her. This wasn't a joke. Sofia had made it cruel.

Waiters had already set an extra place and Anna slipped into her seat.

Silent.

The whole room was silent, staring at them, at her.

Anna remembered to breathe, focused her attention briefly on the gleaming silver cutlery before she lifted her gaze and stitched a practiced, social smile on her mouth. Sofia revelled in attention. Always had, always would. For Anna, it was torture.

She could already feel the trickle of sweat at the base of her spine.

And she didn't know anyone at the table.

Seconds stretched, pulling at Anna's already taut nerves. She deconstructed the intricate fold of her napkin. Zach could at least introduce her.

"This is Gregory's sister-in-law," he said, rearranging his own napkin. "Anna Shrewsbury."

A waiter poured wine, murmured something to Zach and then vanished.

"Sofia's sister?"

Anna stopped feeling sorry for Zach in that instant. She held the speaker's heated gaze, felt the man sizing her up in comparison to her sister. The linen napkin covered her thighs.

For that, she was very grateful. However, Sofia's *reputation* covered her too. Men made assumptions. "Yes."

The man's attention slid from her to Zach. "So, known each other long?"

"Yes."

Zach had paused. She could imagine the anger surging behind that civilised façade.

Tough.

She had been mauled once too often.

Anna's fingers closed around the wineglass. It was better she admit that than have the man sitting next to her grope her leg through what remained of the meal.

The wine was cold and tart. She focused her attention on that and the square plate the waiter slid in front of her. The warmed scent of orange, red onion, of langoustines artfully arranged made her stomach tighten with hunger.

Yes, breakfast had been a rushed slice of toast and lukewarm coffee.

A trickle of conversation started again around her table.

Fine. Zach wasn't introducing anyone. And they seemed more than happy to stay anonymous.

"No games, Anna."

His soft voice made her fingers press hard around her cutlery. Gooseflesh prickled her skin. But she made herself look up, ignore his stern expression. "No games, Zach." She smiled and pointed her fork at him. "But making people aware whose sister I am?" She turned back to her plate. "That just invites trouble."

"I'm sure under normal circumstances you are able to..." He paused. "...handle...any problem. But this week, that is not an option. Are we clear?"

Her fork speared the flesh of a Dublin bay prawn. "Perfectly." Her attention slid to him. "I'm sure I can abstain for one whole week." The fork slipped into her mouth and with satisfaction, she watched the anger fire through him. Let him imply that she slept with any man who asked her.

She stared back at her plate.

It was a myth she had been weaving around herself for six years.

And it kept her safe.

From him.

℘◌℞

Zach stopped himself from scrubbing at his face.

That Gregory could do this to him.

Him.

No.

He didn't want to think ill of Gregory Brabant. The man had been more than a partner to him over the previous twelve years. He ignored the grief that burned through his gut. No. Not thinking ill of him. But Zach really wanted a *very* sharp word with the old man.

His gaze slid involuntarily over Anna's exquisite profile, her dark, bobbed hair curling under her jaw. Her lips closed around the spoon, her eyes drifting shut and he heard her sigh...

Damn her. She was doing it deliberately.

Zach unclenched his teeth.

A week of this.

Her scent was something gently vanilla mixed with the familiar warm aroma of her skin. It had been years since he had been this close to her for this long. And that denial had sent him slightly insane. That had to be the excuse. Had to be.

He threw his linen napkin onto the table, drawing her unwanted attention. Deep brown eyes held him, sparked with wry humour. "Not to your taste?" Her smile was teasing and Zach found it hard to pull his thoughts away from her lips, remembering how his teeth—

"No." Good. His voice was steady, controlled. He had given up on Anna a long time ago. It was her life. And he, very wisely, had stayed the hell out of it. "But I'm glad to see you've rediscovered eating."

A flash of anger burned through her, staining a blush across her flawless skin. His gut tightened. Damn it, he had to stop goading her but her anger aroused him. It always had.

"It's still early, but I'm thinking of the winter."

And then Andrew Wood took her attention again, fat fingers mauling her shoulder. She gave *him* the same bright smile.

Gregory had to be laughing himself into fits.

Gregory had been besotted with his wife, focusing all his attentions onto Sofia, to the exclusion of the business, his friends, everything. But Zach knew Gregory hadn't been totally blind, had been aware of how he...reacted...to his sister-in-law.

No.

Zach put Anna from his mind, tried to find interest in the chatter of the woman to his right, but one thought preoccupied him. This was his father's memorial lunch. He had to keep fixed in his mind how a scheming woman, intent only on money, power and position, had duped and betrayed his father.

And Zach hadn't spoken to his mother in twelve years.

A waiter appeared at Andrew Wood's shoulder, murmuring.

Andrew pushed his chair back. "Would you excuse me? Important phone call."

Zach watched Wood's gaze slide possessively over Anna, a blunt fingertip tracing along her shoulder. He couldn't catch the man's rushed whisper.

"I warned you, Anna..."

She straightened and pulled at the hem of her short jacket. Absently, her fingers played with the white linen napkin still covering her legs. She looked up and her eyes were bright, sharp. Her lips pursed, before she said, "He's just offering what men always offer."

Her words were a kick to his gut. "Really?"

"You should know."

She smiled up at the waiter who poured her coffee, then drank the steaming, black liquid. Her eyes closed, briefly, before turning back to him. Her lips had reddened with the heat and Zach found it difficult to focus on anything else.

"How much longer is this going to go on?"

He blinked. "Not much longer. Why? Planning an assignation with Andrew?" A scorch of anger burned through him. To imagine that man pawing her... "Need I remind you that your *social calendar* is filled for the next week?"

The slight blush to her cheeks only intensified the burn of red to her mouth. "Not by you, Zach." Brown eyes fixed on him. "Never by you."

His blood thrummed. Her denial perversely intensified his need. He'd been hard from the second he saw her in Petersen's office. The damn woman was going to kill him.

No.

She was right.

And he was taunted by that difficult, bitter lesson.

Still, he couldn't stop himself from saying, "Are you so sure?"

Her eyes darkened. There was a rapid pulse at the base of her throat. The destructive desire for each other still pulsed between them. Always had. Probably always would.

"Yes. I am."

He couldn't help the smile that pulled at his mouth. She sounded so certain. He picked up his coffee and relaxed back into his chair. She couldn't be that naïve. Not anymore. Zach cut out those thoughts. He would not think about *why* she was no longer naïve.

"We have a deal, Anna."

"And you seem to forget that." She put her cup down, refusing a refill from the waiter. Her breathing was unnatural, controlled. Colour still slashed her cheeks. "Neither of us wanted this, Zach."

He knew her too well. She was never as overblown as Sofia, but Anna loved her little fits of pique. "Oh, I'm sure you're just making the best of a bad situation." He followed the path Andrew Wood had taken. "And you're not using this week to...fish."

She was also staring at the doors. The colour deepened in her cheeks and her gaze dropped to her coffee cup. A finger traced the white rim. "He said—"

"I don't need the details, Anna."

She closed her eyes. Long lashes brushed her cheeks and Zach was surprised to see the delicate veins in her eyelids. He ignored the twist in his gut. It made her look vulnerable. Anna? Vulnerable? A wry smile pulled at his mouth. The woman really did have every trick.

"Zach..."

That tremble in her voice. His mouth flattened. He could feel the lies brewing. "What?"

She winced. "I want..."

Her dark eyes were extra bright. His chest tightened. Was she going to cry? Oh, Sofia had taught her sister well. "What, Anna?"

Her gaze dropped again. "What he just said..." She took a deep breath. "I need to—"

"No!"

He did not want to know what she *needed* from a man like Andrew Wood.

"Fine." Anna put her napkin on the table. "If you'll excuse me."

"Where are you going?"

Brown eyes, angry, bright, held him. "I'm sure Gregory would allow me to go to the ladies on my own."

And she was gone.

Zach watched her leave the room, weaving through the tables, her long, lithe form, clad in that amazing red, reflected and re-reflected in the suite's many mirrors. The sway of her hips. And that skirt. It revealed an utterly indecent amount of perfect, pale thigh.

Too many others followed her progress.

His jaw tightened.

Damn it.

Anna's affect on him should've been a relic of his past.

"Zach, we have to go..." His father's cousin broke into his thoughts.

Yes, his guests were starting to leave.

Zach struggled to his feet, had to focus on them, smile, agree with their comments about how wonderful his father had been, how he was still sorely missed. Guilt tugged at him. It was his father's memorial lunch. That's where his mind should be. Not trapped by the thoughts of Anna.

He had to look at his watch. Fifteen minutes.

What was she doing?

He scanned the room. But it was just him and the usual die-hard stragglers.

Normally, he relaxed, chatted with remaining people, arranged to move onto the bar. He looked at his watch again. Twenty minutes.

And Andrew Wood hadn't returned either.

His gut was tight.

The woman would not jeopardise his rightful share of the company.

He was in the quiet of the corridor before he realised he'd moved. He buttoned his jacket, smoothed his hand over his tie. There was the chatter of the people behind him and soft shoes on the thick carpet. Anna?

No.

"Can I help you, Mr. Quinn?"

"Ah..." He paused. He needed to find her. He expelled a slow breath. "Have you seen one of my guests? A tall woman, dressed in red?"

The porter's polite façade didn't slip and he pointed back along the corridor. "I believe I saw her and a gentleman—"

Zach was running. The bloody woman would not embarrass him. Not today. Especially not today. He stopped when he burst into the foyer. Steady breaths, his gaze everywhere. The porters were busy with newly arrived customers...too many doors, staircases, alcoves—

There.

The unmistakeable flash of that red suit.

Outside the lifts. With Andrew Wood.

A raw surge of fury powered him forward. To think that once he'd wanted this woman. Zach crushed those thoughts. No. He had saved himself from another very public scandal.

Anna was poison.

Yes. And his for the week.

His hands curled into bloodless fists.

But when this was over, he would never see her again. Ever.

&OCR;

"Leaving so soon, Andrew?" Zach's arm wound around her waist, fingers tight.

Anna released a slow breath. She had been monumentally stupid. She hadn't flirted with Andrew Wood during lunch. She hadn't. She'd just been polite and hoped that Zach would misconstrue that attention. Which he had.

Good. Fine. She would try anything that kept him at arm's length.

But then Andrew made his vile suggestion. And it had hit her. How people viewed her. How she had played into that view, thinking it protected her from Zach.

But nothing, nothing would protect her from him. Not anymore.

She had tried to tell Zach, needed to tell him. However, Zach was his usual self. Completely uninterested in her telling the truth. She'd run, hoping to find a place away from him to gather her courage.

Then Andrew had cornered her coming out of the ladies. All but hustled her through the hotel to the lifts. She would have a bruise on her arm from his meaty fingers and the fact that she had just wrenched herself free.

And now Zach was here to see the fallout.

Stupid tears burned her eyes.

She couldn't blame Gregory for this. Her life was already a mess of lies, a tangle that had caught her up for six years. One she felt impossible to undo. No, she couldn't go on like this. In a week, she would be free. Free of Sofia, of...of Zach. She ignored the constriction in her chest. There were no feelings there for him. None.

She would be free to start over.

Anna looked up at the hard line of Zach's jaw, found his attention fixed on Andrew Wood. Yes. She could start now. "Are you ready to leave?"

"Yes."

"Anna and I had plans," the other man said.

She met Andrew's hot gaze, holding down the familiar shudder. "No. We didn't."

"Why, you..."

Her face burned at the names Andrew Wood called her, his features angry, twisted, but she didn't look away.

"Enough." Zach's low growl sent a chill over her skin. Andrew Wood's face blanched and he took a back step. "Anna is with me."

Andrew stabbed at the lift button. His gaze slid over Anna, his mouth sliding into a sneer. "You're welcome to her."

"Zach—"

"I have people waiting for me."

He turned and strode away. Anna, in a half run, followed him, her boots clicking over the marble floor. The damn things were designed for sitting down, not actually walking. "Zach. Wait!"

He stopped in the quiet of the corridor. "What?"

"I wasn't...I didn't...with him." Her hand waved back down the corridor. She took a steadying breath. Yes. Time for the truth with Zach. Her heart was pounding. There would never be anything between them. Not anymore. It would be her first step to freeing herself of her old life. "It's all a lie."

His gaze narrowed on her. "A lie?"

"Yes. The men. There's been no one." She could feel the fire in her face as she focused on his tie. "No one...since you."

Silence. For too many heartbeats, complete silence.

And then he started to laugh. A harsh, bitter sound. He lifted her chin and his smile was sharp. "You don't need to charm me, Anna. We have this week. After that you can sell off your inheritance and leave the country."

He moved closer. Fingers snaked around her neck.

Her heart was tight. He hadn't believed her. Why had she expected he would?

Zach's breath, warm over her mouth, so close she could almost taste him.

"But don't ever embarrass me like that again." His voice was no more than a rough whisper, his eyes dark, hard. "Because you don't want me as an enemy, Anna."

"I—"

"No." His fingers slid from her skin and chilled air washed away the heat. Anna shivered. "I've had enough lies from you today."

And he left her standing there.

Her hand covered her mouth and she felt the sting of tears. She had finally worked up the guts to tell him the truth and he'd laughed in her face.

The day couldn't get any worse.

Damn.

Sofia would be home now.

Yes. It could.

Chapter Four

Anna caught up with him in the long corridor that led back to the function room. She was not going to try again. He could believe her. Or not. Damn the man. She let out a measured breath and willed her heart to be calm. "Are you ready to leave, now?"

Zach didn't slow his fast stride. "No."

Anna hissed against the pain in her feet. Stupid boots.

"I am not changing my schedule for you."

"Oh, but it's fine for me to chase around after you, wasting my
time—"

Zach stopped. Anna teetered on her heels and found her balance. "Yes."

She gritted her teeth and pushed down the surge of anger that wanted to slap him into next week. "Zach, I really need—"

"What?" His voice was cold and his body stiff. "What lies do you want to spin now, Anna?"

She breathed in. And out. "I've finished with lying."

He laughed again, without mirth. "Of course you have. Lying to you is as easy as breathing. It always has been."

She swallowed the pained lump in her throat. "Not anymore."

"Anna." His hand framed her jaw, tangled in her hair. The heat of his touch burned her skin. "Women have lied to me my whole life. It's what you do."

A fist crushed in her gut. She was just another one in a long line. She stepped back beyond his touch. "No."

A smile quirked his mouth. "Then we'll agree to disagree."

"Fine." She sidestepped him and pushed open the door to the ladies. "What? Can I not go to the toilet now?"

"Again?"

"Yes." Regret sparked into the familiar burn of anger. The man could turn her emotions faster than anyone she had ever known. She lifted her hand, stared at her palm and then waved it at him. "Or would you prefer to meet your colleagues with a red welt across your jaw?"

Zach laughed, something harsh and grating. "You're enjoying this latest mask, aren't you?" He glanced ahead. "I'll be in the bar. And you have ten minutes, Anna. Any longer and I'll come in there and get you."

"How will that look to your precious reputation?"

He ignored her and strode away. His words cut back. "Ten minutes, Anna."

She let the door bang into place.

Anna released a shallow breath and slumped into the nearest chair. It was the one she had vacated no more than half an hour before. A smile tugged at her mouth and she ran her hand through her hair. "How am I going to last the day, never mind the week?"

She stared up at the white ceiling and breathed the soft scent of jasmine deep into her lungs. She blinked. She knew that scent.

A stall door hinge creaked.

Anna jumped. No. It was not the best time to be talking to herself.

She stood. Her heels clicked over the polished floor and she stopped before the gleaming sink. She stared at her reflection, willing herself to find the courage to be in Zach's company again. But her insides rioted.

"Anna, this is a surprise."

The knot in her chest twisted tighter. Jasmine. "Isabelle."

Isabelle Quinn put her bag onto the table. She turned the golden taps and washed her hands, drying them with slow, measured wipes on the small towel. She dropped it into the basket.

Turning back to the mirror, Isabelle examined her reflection. Long nails traced over her perfect jaw line, her head tilted to the sharp spotlights above. Her hair was a sheet of gleaming copper. She pulled at a strand, before stroking it back into place.

"I didn't expect you to be here today." Anna twitched a smile. Getting out, finding Zach and telling him his ex-wife was prowling sounded like a great plan right then. She was certain he would want to avoid a confrontation. Anna waved a hand back to the door. "I should be going..."

"Zachary's waiting for you?"

"Yes."

Isabelle smiled.

Anna ignored the kick to her gut. Zach's ex-wife was flawlessly beautiful.

"You know I've always tried to help you." Isabelle's smile softened. "I tried to warn you years ago to stay away from him. Zachary enjoys mind games." She turned back to her reflection and tilted her jaw. Without looking, she opened her bag and pulled out a gold compact. She dabbed powder over her skin. "Don't fall for his charm, Anna. I did." For a moment, her smooth brow wrinkled. Her lips twitched and the furrow slid away. "Thankfully, I saw sense early on."

Anna was about to say that, obviously, there was nothing between her and Zach. The constraints of Gregory's will stopped her. And there was the lie. Because something did seethe between them, had for too many years. "Yes." She pushed back her cuff and stared at her watch. There had to be only a few minutes before Zach came looking for her. "It was nice seeing you again, Isabelle—"

"We've always been friends." She put her hand on Anna's arm and her fingers tightened. "I'm not Sofia."

Anna let out a slow breath and she made the smile work across her mouth. "I know."

She had always admired Isabelle's poise, her innate charm. When Anna was younger she had tried to be her. And for a short time, Isabelle had been the big sister she had never had, one with whom to share her worries and secrets.

Anna's smile eased into something more real as she said, "It was kind of you to sit with me that afternoon. Especially when you had your own problems."

Isabelle turned back to the mirror. "My decree absolute." She brushed a delicate sheen of gloss over her lips. "To be honest, your miserable boyfriend took my mind off it. Zachary and I had ended long before then. It was odd to be so...disturbed by it."

Isabelle had been his wife and Anna had never understood his animosity. Anna focused on the taps and ignored the twist of guilt. It made her uneasy. Always had. "Iain Bridger. I was his girlfriend for a whole week and then he broke my heart. Left me for Fiona Campbell. The whole running off, getting soaked to the skin and excessive tears was a slight overreaction on my part."

Isabelle grinned. "You were sixteen. It's what you do at that age."

Anna couldn't help her laugh. "True."

"And now you're what, twenty-five?" Isabelle packed her cosmetics back into her bag. "Zachary will hurt you far more than Iain Bridger."

"I'm not..." Anna stopped herself. "He won't."

"I thought that too." Isabelle turned her body and smoothed her hands down the soft silk of her pale blue, shift dress. "He's not what he appears to be." For a second, her mouth turned down in a hard line. "Not what I thought he was anyway." Her calm expression returned and Anna doubted what she thought she'd seen. A malicious gleam lit Isabelle's pure green eyes and she looked too much like Sofia for comfort. "And of course, then there's his problem—"

"Anna. Your time is up."

The door banged against the floor stop.

Zach stared. Isabelle. What other nightmares could the day conjure? Anna looked pink and she wouldn't meet his eye. Or couldn't. A fist crushed tight in his chest. Isabelle had been at work again. "Hello, Isabelle."

"Zachary." She smiled. He was no longer fooled by the pleasing perfection of her face. "How nice to see you again. I didn't realise the date."

"Of course." He stood back from the doorway and indicated for Anna to precede him. "Anna, please."

Isabelle's smile deepened. Her heels clacked against the polished marble and Zach willed himself to breathe evenly. Her finger edged his jaw. Skin prickled where she touched and he forced down the need to flinch. "I love the way you become monosyllabic around me." She glanced back to the unmoving Anna. "Remember what I said."

Anna's cheeks flushed a deeper pink.

"You used to come looking for me too, Zachary. So possessive." Her gaze slid down his chest, dropped lower and a sharp smile curled her mouth. "But then that all changed."

"Yes." He stepped away from her, stood between her and Anna. "I'm sure *someone's* missing you, Isabelle."

"Harsh."

"True."

"Zach." Anna's cool hand slipped into his and her fingers brushed his palm. Heat shot up his arm. "We should go."

"Isabelle." He stepped forward and out into the thankfully empty corridor. There was enough gossip circulating about him today. He wanted to get away. It seemed Anna read his thoughts.

"Let's get out of here, Zach."

Her words perversely strengthened his resolve to stay. He pulled his hand free of hers and increased his pace. "Neither you, nor her, will drive me out of here."

"You're being ridiculous!"

"I liked you better as a liar."

He strode ahead of her and his breath tightened. His mouth ran off before his brain engaged. Always did around Anna. He was an idiot. "Anna..."

"No." Her face had flushed. "And Isabelle worried about me falling for your charm."

Isabelle. The thought of his ex-wife spreading her lies to Anna had pain shooting into his skull. He rubbed a hand over the back of his neck. "I don't need to remind you of the stipulations of Gregory's will."

"Thank you, Zach." She pushed open the glass doors leading into the bar. "It's obviously so difficult to remember."

Zach stopped himself from pinching the bridge of his nose. A headache pulsed and mixed with the wine, worsening his mood. He leant against the bar and ordered two mineral waters.

Anna curved an eyebrow.

"Do you really want anything more to drink?"

"Around you?" She put her tiny, impractical bag on the polished counter. "Unwise."

"Funny."

The doors opened again and Isabelle stood there. Zach counted the seconds as she waited for everyone in the crowded bar to look at her. And they did. Isabelle was, after all, a striking woman. He turned back to his drink, his fingertip sliding down the cold, wet glass. Nine years wasn't long enough to separate them. A twist of a smile curved his mouth.

"What?" Anna glanced at him briefly and sipped at her water.

All thought of Isabelle faded.

Anna's skin glowed in the clear light. It was as if someone had kicked him in the chest. He saw his hand moving to frame her jaw. His fingers slid over the delicate skin of her cheek. He was stupid to keep touching her, but this was Anna. He couldn't stop.

"Zach..."

His thumb pressed against her lip, brushing away the moisture. Silencing her.

This woman had his life in a tailspin. His privacy, his reputation, meant everything to him. Always had. But they were forgotten as easily as his ex-wife. He slid from his barstool and edged closer. Anna's parted thighs brushed against his legs. Her mouth was level with his. So close, he could almost taste her.

Anna's eyes were a liquid black, endless, and with each breath, he felt himself falling, falling—

"Anna Shrewsbury!"

Zach's hand dropped. It was a spell that she cast over him. He would touch her and forget that she was exactly like his Isabelle. No. Lust would not make him a fool for a second time.

A stool scraped over the floor and Zach shook the haze from his mind. "Excuse me, we're not—" He stared and he knew his face slid into the familiar ice mask. His gut twisted and he stopped his hands from tightening into fists. "Nathan."

The wide bright smile flared Zach's growing irritation. Smug. The bastard always looked smug. "Zachary."

"We were having a private conversation."

"Conversation? That what you call it?" With a smirk, Nathan Alexander planted himself on the stool and patted Anna's leg. She twisted away from his touch. "Haven't seen Anna for years."

"Yes, there's a reason for that."

A hard edge cut her voice and it made heat rush under Zach's skin. Lead settled in his stomach. Nathan was a man from her past. Yes, history was repeating itself. "Nathan." He kept his voice low. Already, those closest to them had grown still and he could feel them listening. "So how much of a hint do you need to go away?" Fury burned through him. With a slow breath, he contained it. "And I'm being polite."

"Zachary." His oily tones made Zach want to grab him by his ridiculously expensive jacket and haul him up against the nearest wall. "I understand you're stressed today. But we can be mature about this? I just wanted to say hello to Anna."

"Done," Anna said. "Bye."

Zach's mouth twitched. "Now that's both of us."

His pretty-boy lips turned down and a crease formed on Nathan's too-smooth brow. "Isabelle wants to talk to you in private."

"I have nothing to say to her."

Nathan sank against the shallow back of the stool. He watched Zach while he swirled his whiskey, the ice clinking against the crystal. "We both know Isabelle." There was a conscious flick of his eyes to Anna. Zach frowned. "I'll keep Anna company."

"Two minutes." He pushed himself away from the bar. Habit made him straighten and fasten his jacket. "Anna."

"Counting the seconds."

Zach drew in a deep breath and turned through the loose crowd. He should have been spending the afternoon in the quiet company of his friends. Instead, he had his ex-wife, her lover...and most aggravating of all, Anna.

Isabelle relaxed back in a curved, leather booth. A hard little smile cut her mouth. He stared down at her. Her beauty was all surface, he knew that now. But he'd been a shallow young man when he proposed. He had learnt his lesson. He never trusted a pretty face again. "All right. What?"

"Sometimes I don't know what I saw in you. What Anna sees in you." She waved a manicured hand at the empty curve of the rest of her booth. "Sit."

"Anna and I are not open for discussion."

Isabelle stared past him and her elegant features tightened. He refused to turn. He did not want to see Nathan and Anna together. Old memories fired his reluctance.

"Lust suits you, Zachary." She sipped wine and her tongue tip touched her wet lips. "But then I always thought it did."

Was she flirting with him? The thought made his skin itch. "Get to the point."

She patted the place beside her. Her French polished talons gleamed against the dark brown leather. "Sit."

Zach pulled up a short stool, unfastened his jacket and sat. "Two minutes."

"You never used to be so much of a stickler for your schedule."

"I didn't have to before I met you. One and half minutes."

Isabelle's perfect lips pursed. Her jaw stiffened. "You and Anna are an unlikely couple."

Zach said nothing. He willed his expression to stone.

"Especially given our past."

"One minute."

Loathing darkened her green eyes. "I told her."

Cold rippled through him. He watched the loathing transform to satisfaction. A wrinkle cut her flawless cheek from her sneer of a smile, marring her beauty. "Your time is up." Zach stood.

"Aren't you going into your rant now? Threatening my alimony payments?"

He'd had enough of continually playing her games. Zach smiled and some of the surety slipped from Isabelle's face. He shrugged. "Spin your lies."

Isabelle's gaze travelled over his body and ice prickled his skin. "Are they lies?"

Zach wasn't listening. His attention fixed on Anna. Nathan Alexander leant against the bar, half-blocking the woman from his view. But he couldn't miss her smile. Curving bright. Relaxed. There was that hitch in his chest again. But history was not repeating itself. He wasn't the same man who had fallen for Isabelle's lies twelve years before. That fool was long gone.

Isabelle's sharp voice sliced into this thoughts. "Your reputation always meant more to you than any woman."

"I can control my reputation." *Trust it.* But those words went unsaid.

Isabelle laughed. "Is that why you pay everyone off?"

"You've had more than enough of my time."

"Shame I won't be there when she laughs in your face." The leather of her seat creaked, but Zach didn't turn to look at her. Anna's tilted head and the keen look of interest forced another twist of the knife in his gut. "Anna Shrewsbury? You can't help yourself." She paused. "You really are your father's son."

It was hard to believe that he had once loved Isabelle, loved her and married her. "Collect Nathan." He smoothed his hand down over his tie, his jacket. "I think you have to leave now."

"Zachary..."

He turned and the satisfaction slid from her face. "Now."

Isabelle rose with her usual grace and her chin lifted as she met his glare. Her green eyes were hard. "Your reputation rules you." She presented him with a brittle smile and then looked to Anna. "And hers trails after her like slime." Her hand stroked over his jaw and he cursed the natural flinch. "I'm an angel compared to her." She patted his cheek. "And you know it."

"Bye, Isabelle."

A loose crowd of men parted before her. A wry smile tugged at Zach's mouth when hot looks followed her consciously swaying hips. But Isabelle wasn't his concern anymore. Anna was. For this week, at least.

He let out a slow breath and made himself follow Isabelle.

ဆဝ

Anna gripped her glass and smiled until her face ached.

Nathan Alexander. Another man who she didn't want to see again.

He was a friend of Sofia's and had been a plague in her late teens. Too smooth and plastic-pretty, he made her skin crawl. But she smiled. Because he had said that if she didn't, he would tell Zach about them.

"No need to grimace, Anna."

She sipped at the water in her glass, the melting ice clinking. It stopped her from telling him what she really wanted to say. The cold run of water cooled her. "I don't like being blackmailed."

Nathan ran his fingertip around the edge of Zach's glass. It hummed. "It's not blackmail."

"No. Of course not." Her knuckles whitened around her own glass. "You just plan to lie to the man I'm with—"

Nathan held up his hand. "No lies, Anna." Her hand itched to wipe the smirk off his face. "You propositioned me."

"I did not!"

"Anna, I have to go." Isabelle glanced back to Zach's implacable face and she caught the swift slide of the woman's regret. "Nathan."

The man took Anna's hand and pressed it to his lips. His pale eyes fixed on her. She shuddered. "Goodbye, my luscious Anna."

Anna forced her breathing into an even rhythm. He would bait her to the last. He put Isabelle's arm through his and with a flicking wave from Zach's ex-wife, they left.

She expelled a hot breath. "Creep."

"I see you know Nathan Alexander well."

Zach settled himself back onto his stool and picked up his drink. Distaste cut his mouth and he waved for the bartender to get him a fresh glass. Anna didn't know whether that was meant to be a joke so she sipped at her water again and said, "Can we go now?" She straightened. "Or do you want more bad memories to crawl out?"

He shrugged. "The entire company has the whole day off." He picked the damp napkin from the bottom of the glass and dropped it back on the counter. "I have nowhere else to be."

"I do."

A smile twisted. "So..." She was the focus of those steel blue eyes. "How do you know Nathan so well?"

Anna ignored the edge to his voice. "Like I know everyone. He's one of Sophia's hangers-on."

"Ah, Sophia."

"And what's that supposed to mean?" Anna was tired of the games. Her head was starting to ache. "Look, Zach." She picked up her bag. "I'm leaving. I think it's time I dictated some of our time together."

"Anna..."

"Want to make another scene, Zach?"

His usual cold, unyielding expression settled across his face. It was little wonder that Isabelle had broken away from Zach. The man had the emotional range of a stump.

"Go where?"

The tight pain in her chest eased. "I want to get back to Ashford, pack and go without seeing Sofia."

"Fine." He put his empty glass back on the bar. "Then we go."

Anna blinked. "Just like that?"

"The less I see of Sofia today the better."

Her smile was sharp before she turned to the door. "Snap!" she said.

Chapter Five

The car door clunked shut.

It was four o'clock, still just enough time for Anna to be in and out of the house before her sister was any the wiser. Zach slid onto the backseat beside her. He grimaced and pulled out his phone.

"Quinn." His face darkened. "Now?"

Anna tugged at her seat belt and tried not to listen to the rushed voice on the other end of the mobile. Her stomach knotted. The rich food from the dinner still burned. From Zach's tight expression, it didn't look good. This was *not* her day.

"Fine." He paused. His voice softened. "Thank you, Elise." A sharp stab of his thumb ended the call. "David. The office."

"I thought we were..." Anna began.

"You thought wrong," Zach muttered and yanked his seat belt across his chest. "Seems Gregory's little game isn't all that private, after all."

"I don't understand."

His gaze gripped her and Anna willed herself not to shrink away. "Don't you?" The car pulled out into afternoon traffic, smooth, silent. "Dalton suddenly wants a meeting. He's heard disturbing rumours about company infighting."

"Should I know who this Dalton is?"

Zach's sharp profile silhouetted against the window. "He's wealthy. Of course you do."

Anna straightened her skirt and refused to be drawn. Yet, she had the uncomfortable suspicion he was right. The name did sound familiar. Nothing would make her admit that, though.

They crawled through Friday afternoon traffic with Anna's spine tense and aching. She wanted to be home, packing. Have the time to avoid the snide comments of her sister, to prepare herself for the exhibition. Yet, here she was sitting in an air-conditioned car with a man who hated her, heading to a meeting that could take hours.

Definitely not how she had seen the day progressing.

"Here's fine, David," Zach murmured and the car pulled smoothly to the kerb.

Anna tottered onto the pavement and stared up at the stunning glass façade of the Head Office of Quinn Brabant Technologies. This was another place she hadn't visited in years. One stupid act had completely changed how she lived her life.

Belatedly, she followed Zach up the wide, marble steps. Large doors slid back with a faint hiss.

Her boots clacked over the marble floor. The atrium was still as breathtaking, stretching high, the roof a mesh of gleaming glass. Trees rustled in the air-conditioning, spreading the gentle scent of new leaves. Memory swamped her. Being fourteen and her first meeting with Gregory, riding in the glass-fronted lift to the top floor and finding not an ogre, but a friend.

Anna's hand covered her mouth and she took a slow breath.

"Are you scared of heights?"

The lift door closed.

"No," Anna muttered. She forced her hand to her side and willed back the burn of tears. Of course, this building had other memories. Trapped in the lift with Zach, Anna pushed them from her mind.

The lift doors opened onto a silent office. Anna ignored the little burst of panic. She wasn't alone with Zach. He had a client to meet. The scent of polish and clean carpets pushed her mind back.

She was nineteen again and getting out of the lift to attend her first Christmas party. They walked past dark, empty desks to the far side of the sprawling office. Food, alcohol, music and chatter flowed.

Sophia had refused to attend. It was a more relaxed affair, not the expensive pomp she had demanded year in, year out. Therefore, Anna was Gregory's guest.

"So you're here in Sophia's stead?"

"Yes." Butterflies massed in her stomach and that was just ridiculous. This was Zach. Boring, stiff, annoying Zach. She stared into the fizzing glass of champagne. Two sips couldn't make her feel this giddy. "She...wasn't feeling too well."

"Of course she wasn't. She never does." He lounged against the wall, an untouched drink in his hand. His cultured voice came out of the shadows and why it made her breath hitch she couldn't explain. This was Zach. "And little Anna has stepped into her big sister's shoes for the first time." A thumb tip stroked along her jaw. "Haven't you?"

"Have I?"

His low chuckle sent the butterflies whirling. "Who are you out to catch tonight?"

Anna blinked. The slide of his thumb over her skin was almost hypnotic and she leant into his touch. "Gregory only asked me yesterday."

"And you just happened to have this dress"—his fingers trailed down the sensitive skin of her throat, caressed the thin strap clinging to her bare shoulder—"languishing in your wardrobe."

Her chest hurt with held breath and a liquid ache pulsed through her blood. What was he doing to her? "It's just a dress."

"On anyone else but you, Anna."

Heat burst under her skin. He was teasing her, inflicting a cruel joke. Anna jerked back from his touch. She could still feel the imprint of him on her skin. "Don't make fun of me, Zach."

"Anna." His glass clattered down onto a nearby table. Warm hands framed her face, the sudden contact making her gasp. Shadows carved his face and darkened eyes held her. "This is not a joke."

And he kissed her.

She crushed down more memories.

She'd been a young, inexperienced idiot.

Zach strode ahead. With her heels sinking into the thick carpet, she followed him. He disappeared through a door. But there was no client. Her nails dug hard at her palms. She watched Zach drop the blinds to the glass-panelled room.

"What...what are you doing?"

Zach's laugh was bitter. "Don't worry, Anna, I have no interest in seeing you spread across this table." The sharp glitter of his eyes made the nails bite harder. "Not right now, anyway."

He grabbed a remote, pressed a button and a screen slid down from the ceiling. He pressed more buttons and the screen flared into life. "Sit there," he said, pointing to the corner. "Out of sight."

"Please wouldn't kill you," Anna muttered.

"Please, Anna," he said, his tone unchanged.

"And you call me impolite."

"Damn it, Anna, this is important." He expelled a harsh breath. "*Please* sit in that corner chair and *please* be quiet."

The man was infuriating. Anna plonked herself onto a chair. An afterthought had her fill a cup from the water cooler she sat beside. She sipped the ice-cold water and silently buried daggers in Zach's taut back.

He sank into a chair, absent fingers undoing the buttons of his jacket. He scratched over his hair, but then smoothed tousled strands into place. A cool calmness settled onto his features. He pressed another button.

A man filled the screen. Bluntly handsome with shrewd dark eyes, and yes Zach was right. She knew his face from...somewhere.

"Quinn, what is going on?" the man demanded.

"Nothing has changed."

"Nothing has changed?" The man's face flushed. "You don't even own your own company anymore!"

Zach's face didn't flicker. "We can call the whole thing off right now, if you want Eric."

Water splashed over Anna's legs, freezing her. "Oh my God."

"Who else is there with you, Quinn?"

"No one of importance."

"Really?" His face swallowed up the screen. "Who is it?"

That odd-shaped mole above his right eyebrow. Anna winced. Eric Dalton. One of the most paranoid men on the planet. He was also one of Sophia's admirers. Was she the source of Zach's leak?

Zach let out a slow sigh. "Let Mr. Dalton see you, Anna."

Maybe he wouldn't recognise her. Maybe he'd been too drunk when he'd made that pass to remember the fact that she'd poured a drink over his head.

Dark eyes narrowed. "Anna Shrewsbury."

No. Of course, he remembered. She gave a half-hearted wave. "Hello, Eric."

"No one important, Quinn?" Eric Dalton's laughter was harsh. "I don't think the infamous Anna Shrewsbury qualifies as that."

Zach's jaw tightened. "I thought you two would be acquainted."

"With the luscious Anna? Isn't everyone?"

Heat scorched Anna's face. "You're most definitely not, Eric."

The man sat back in his chair. Sharp light cut across his heavy features. A smile tugged at his lip. "Now that's just being cruel, Anna." His gaze flickered and she knew then that he was lying to annoy Zach.

"I poured water over your head."

"Anna..." His oily tone made her skin crawl. "You don't have to pretend in front of Zach. He's known you even longer than I have."

Anger burned a fire through her gut. "Since you seem determined to lie about me"—Anna jabbed her thumb at the door—"I'll be outside."

She closed the door on his laughter. Damn the man. She'd dug a deep hole for herself with her numerous lies. Her reputation...well, she didn't want to dwell on how others saw her. But it had been made very obvious to her that day.

Anna stared down into the atrium. She calmed her breathing. There was little use in getting so angry. Zach would continue to believe she jumped anything with a big enough wallet. She doubted Eric Dalton's lies could blacken her name any further.

Though she did hope Zach could think she would have more taste.

Anna snorted and ran a hand through her hair.

She leant back against a pillar, glancing around the desks and cubes. Until she found *that* corner. Her lips burned again at the memory and she tried to think of something, anything else.

But the past was too strong.

He tasted of brandy and another, indefinable taste that almost made her groan. The gentle pressure of his lips, savouring her. His hands slipped from her face, shaped her shoulders, arms until he found the glass clutched tight in her hand. It found a new home on a convenient desk.

She was insane. This was Zach. Zach whose hands trailed fire down her body in slow exploration.

"I wanted to do this from the moment I saw you tonight."

His voice was a heated whisper against her skin and it pulsed a need through Anna that she'd never experienced. Her spine pressed up against the cool plaster of a pillar, Zach's body deliciously pinning her. "Why?" *The word was almost a gasp.*

His mouth found hers, pulling slow, soft kisses that had her head spinning.

"How could I not?"

It wasn't an answer, but at that moment she didn't care. His tongue flickered against her lips, her teeth and with her heart slamming, she opened her mouth to him.

The deliberate sweep of Zach's tongue over hers, hot, intense. This was unreal. Completely...

He deepened the kiss and all thought scattered.

Anna threaded her fingers through his hair, pressing his mouth hard against hers. Zach groaned. His hands shaped her waist and slid lower, curving over her hip and gripping her behind.

The rub of his erection against her body sparked little pulses of pleasure. Her hips shifted and heat flared. She groaned and her hands moved down, holding him to her.

"Do you know what you're doing to me, Anna?" Zach's heated breath stirred her skin and she shivered. His leg nudged hers, eased them apart. "What do you want?"

"You."

The word gasped out on too little air. The hard pressure of his leg ground against her pubic bone and liquid heat melted through her body. She found his mouth again.

More. She had to have more of him. Now.

Faster.

Harder.

Fire burned up from her pelvis, her body tight, aching—

Light exploded behind her eyes and Zach swallowed her sighing moan.

Her kisses slowed. Zach supported her against the pillar as pleasure loosened her body, her legs. Her head fell back.

"Anna."

His voice, suddenly sharp.

"Anna."

With a start, she jumped out of the past. Her body was edgy, the need to be satisfied an unrelenting throb. A trembling hand wiped at her mouth and she willed herself to look at him. "Have...have you finished?"

That steel blue gaze drilled her. "Have you?"

"What?"

"Seeing Dalton again..." His finger stroked her hot cheek and his touch was electric. She couldn't hold back the gasp. His gaze narrowed. "...has obviously turned you on."

Anna shuddered and stepped away from him. "I don't think so." She let out a slow breath. "I need to get home, Zach. If I have to pack and get ready for tonight, it's not leaving me much time."

"So if I did this..."

The ached for burn of his mouth scorched over hers. His hands coursed her ribs, hips and for an insane second she let her body mould itself to his. This was so much better than pale memory. The solid feel of him under her searching hands. The angry clash of lips, tongues, teeth. Anna rubbed herself against the solid length of his erection, stoking the fire in her blood. God, she wanted him. She had always wanted him.

"...you'd take me right here."

The raw growl against her skin jerked her back. Sense crashed into her dazed brain. Rage and desire warred in his eyes and Anna's insides shrivelled. Why him? Why did she want a man who despised her?

"Not today, Zach."

"You can't help yourself, Anna."

"And neither, it seems, can you."

Zach hated the fact that she was right.

Dalton's fat, smirking face still burned in his mind. That and what he had muttered when Anna banged the office door. "Such a feisty girl. I enjoyed her, immensely."

Zach had wanted to slam Dalton's head through a wall.

His gaze raked over her pale face. He fought the insatiable need to have her, the very real ache that demanded he bury himself in her and make her forget that other men existed. This wasn't him. His gut knotted. Hadn't been for six, very long years. "Let's get out of here." He waved her on towards the lifts.

"I never slept with that odious man."

"This subject is closed." He didn't want to find himself wrapped in more of her lies, not when he was stuck in a lift with her. The subtle hints of vanilla, the clean scent of her skin caught in the air and still lingered on his tongue. The taunting ache in his body was almost unbearable.

"I'm telling you the truth. He's not. Eric Dalton's a close friend of Sophia. I met him three years ago. He...he propositioned me. I poured a jug of iced water over his head."

"I'm not discussing it, Anna."

"Fine." She presented him with her back. "You're obviously not familiar with the truth."

"From you? I have no idea."

Had that been a little gasp? Zach wished he could find the solitude of his apartment. Maybe then he could be calm and rational about Anna. A sour laugh echoed in his mind. But then, nothing about Anna had ever made him feel sane.

"Did he say I was good?"

"Anna."

She turned and her dark brown eyes were bright and hard. "Did he? Did he go into detail? Is that what fired *you* up, Zach?"

"No!"

She stood so close he could almost feel the imprint of her body over his. Her gaze slid down. "Are you sure?" Her finger toyed with his belt buckle. Zach's blood pounded. "And how do I know you're telling the truth?" Her fleeting caress of the bulge in his trousers made him expel a sharp hiss. She stepped back.

The lift doors opened. Her smile was brittle. "Think about who you would rather believe. Me or him."

Zach cursed under his breath and followed her across the marbled atrium.

He had a bloody week of this. It would kill him.

ℰℭ

Zach climbed into the car and sat in a stony silence.

She had to ask. "We're going to Ashford now?"

"You're still living quite happily with your sister then?" His tone was cutting.

"Happily?" Anna held his gaze, but the ice there made her look away. She stared out of the window, watching the slow-moving, rush-hour traffic. She rubbed at her eyelids. Sofia would be home. "Not yet."

"Why?"

The question surprised Anna. She turned to him...

"What have you promised to deliver?" he asked.

...and found the usual suspicion. It made her tongue sharp. Any truth was wasted on him. "Your fortune, obviously." His eyes sparked and her heart beat faster. Anna was more than happy to fling his own words back at him. "But you'd like to think that of me, wouldn't you?"

"So why haven't you moved out?"

There was the simple reason. "Money," she said, and turned her attention back to the window. Then there was the complicated reason. The one that came with an old pain. Anna had been under her sister's thumb—under her control—for almost as long as she could remember. It was hard to break away.

Zach laughed. "Money? You?"

"Yes, me," she muttered. "Glad to see this amuses you."

"How could it not?"

Anna let out a slow breath. "Look, I think it would be best if you stayed in the car."

"No."

"Zach..."

"I learned my lesson this afternoon." His voice was cold, hard. "I'm not letting you out of my sight."

"Sofia—"

"All the more reason." His eyebrow lifted. "Time to conspire?"

"Fine."

Nerves had her chest tight. Her sister and Zach in the same house. And she thought her day had been horrible enough.

The car crawled through the late afternoon traffic, until finally, Anna started to recognise familiar landmarks.

"Stop here."

The chauffeur's eyes found Zach's and caught that man's brief nod.

She didn't wait for the chauffeur, scrambling out of her seat. Standing, she tugged at her skirt. A high brick wall faced her. Behind it was Ashford's south garden. Anna knew that Sofia liked to relax with some of her cronies in the den around that time. A swift run over manicured lawns would have Anna in the kitchen with no one the wiser.

Zach.

She could feel him behind her.

Her skin prickled.

"What are you doing, Anna?"

She made herself look at him. "Neither of us wants to see Sofia. We go in this way? We don't."

Zach waved his arm, a smile lurking. "Lead on."

Biting back more words, Anna turned. She searched in her jacket pocket for her keys, found them, and turned one into the solid, wooden door.

Hinges creaked. Wood groaned.

Anna winced and put her weight behind the door.

She stumbled forward, cursing the stupid boots. Her heels buried deep into soft, dark earth. A smile twisted her mouth. She hoped Sofia had paid a fortune for them because they were ruined.

Anna closed her eyes. Thinking like her sister. A habit she had to fight.

The garden door clanked shut.

Time to move.

She yanked her boots free of the damp earth and stared over the beauty of the manicured lawn, sunlight picking out the vivid greens, stretching out to lush, flower-thick borders. Gregory's other love, besides her sister, had been his gardens.

And she wouldn't spike it. Leaning against the door, she tugged her boots down, finally pulling them over her tortured toes.

Anna couldn't help the sigh of relief.

She found Zach staring at her. "Gregory loved this stretch of grass."

He blinked.

Anna waved her muddied boots at him. "These would destroy it." He was still staring. "Come on," she muttered. "If we're lucky, Sofia's in the cinema room. That looks out onto the west garden."

The grass was cool under foot, a balm to aching soles. She started to run. A smile broke out across her mouth. The rush in her blood, the joy of it. It had been years since she'd run barefoot...and then memories surfaced. Her brief childhood with her parents, exploring Middleton's acres like a semi-wild thing—

"Anna!"

She raced for the open doors that led into the kitchen. Let the oh-so-correct and starch-stiff Zachary Quinn blow some fresh air through his lungs. The thought had her grinning. She grabbed at the white-painted doorjamb, swinging to a stop, and laughed.

"What the hell are you doing?"

His sharp eyes sparked with anger. Zach wasn't even out of breath.

"Running, Zach." She straightened and felt the joy of it fizz away. Sofia was probably somewhere in the house. She turned to the shadowed interior, the immaculate kitchen stretching out into the breakfast room. "I used to do it a lot."

His finger curled a lock of hair around her ear.

Anna's skin prickled at the delicate brush of his fingertips over sensitive skin. "Don't, Zach," she murmured, turning her head away. His games hurt and the old, familiar pain pulled tight in her chest.

"Playing hard to get, now? Is this yet another new persona?"

She made herself straighten. He knew the truth now. Something about that made her feel...free. A smile curved her mouth. "What you choose to believe about me is your business."

With that, she turned into the kitchen.

"What I *choose*—"

Zach gripped her upper arm, pulled her towards him. Pressed against him, the solid touch of his body burned against hers. Anna stared up at him, her mouth dried. Lips parted—

"Do you realise how much those boots *cost?*"

Sofia's shrill cry cut through Anna. Damn. Luck never ran with her. Never.

She should be thankful.

Zach stood back. His fingers dropped away.

Sofia snatched at the boots, turning them, painted nails twitching over the clods of black earth still stuck to the expensive leather. She muttered curses under her breath. Hard green eyes fixed on Anna. "This is the thanks I get. You could hardly—"

She saw Zach.

Her sister's face changed. Harsh lines dropped and there was a glitter to Sofia's eyes that worked a tense ache across Anna's shoulders. There it was again. The face that charmed men. Flawless, with a perfection that had passed over Anna.

"Zachary."

Yes. The hard bite to her voice was gone. Sofia was as much a game player as Zach.

"Sofia."

And Zach. Clipped. Cool. The hairs on the back of Anna's neck twitched. The disastrous evening had started early, flowing neatly from the nightmare of the afternoon.

"So you agreed to the plan." Sofia's soft smile curved her mouth and a thin eyebrow lifted.

"As did you." A short pause. "Why?"

Sofia waved a dismissive hand at her sister. "Run along. I need to speak privately. I'm sure there's something you have to do for tonight."

Heat burst over Anna's face. She was being sent away like a child. The thought that she had only until the end of the week put steel in her spine. She was no longer the devastated nine-year-old left with Sofia. "No."

"Anna." Sofia's smile hardened. "This is private."

There was a fist in Anna's stomach. She felt sick. But she made herself hold her sister's gaze. What could she do to her now? Anna felt every tight breath. "You agreed to this. Zach and I are stuck with each other for the week."

Sofia turned and dropped the soiled boots into a bin. The lid clanged shut. "And whose idea do you think that was?"

Anna blinked.

Zach's low laugh made her jump. "Really, Sofia?"

"Of course." Her attention slid from Zach to Anna and back again. "Gregory didn't believe that she wanted that stupid cottage enough...and I said this would be the perfect way." Her richly red mouth twitched. "I knew how much you...don't get on."

"That is a lie." The fist crushed Anna's insides. Gregory wouldn't have said that. He didn't play those sort of games.

"That you don't get on?" Sofia pulled open the large stainless steel fridge and stared over the contents. "I thought it was apparent to everyone."

"Look at me." Anna bit out the words. This was what Sofia did. This was always what she did. "Gregory did not—"

"Anna, believe in your fairy tales. I told you to leave. You wouldn't." Sofia sighed and turned her head. "Go." Her hand flicked. "Slip into one of your comfortable sacks." Her bright green gaze slid over what she wore. "That didn't work. You just can't *carry* fashion."

Anna's face burned. "Your idea of fashion."

"*Anyone's* idea of fashion."

"Are you two finished?" Zach straightened and ran an absent hand over the front of his jacket. "And while I'm thoroughly enjoying this little show..." He turned to Anna. "You have to pack."

Her stomach twisted. A dreadful evening stretched ahead of her...and at its end, she wouldn't be able to escape to the peace, the silence of her little room. No. She had to go with him, with Zach. Go to *that* apartment.

Sofia smirked. "Be gentle with her, Zach."

Anna felt the heat scorch to the roots of her hair. She hadn't seen them in the kitchen just now. And Sofia had never known. She hadn't.

"Enough."

His familiar low growl raised the hairs on Anna's skin. "We're following the rules, Sofia." Her sister's bright red lips pursed under Zach's narrowed gaze. "I suggest you do the same."

"Meaning?"

"No one must know about this...arrangement."

Sofia's mouth twisted into a sarcastic smile. "Oh, you'll earn your inheritance." Her attention returned to the contents of the fridge. She pulled out a chilled bottle of vodka. "If you last."

Zach's fingers closed around Anna's elbow and the jolt of his touch shot through her. Damn it, he was the last man she wanted anywhere near her. Anna wanted to scrub at her face. Of course, he *had* been the last man.

She shrugged herself free.

But found him following her.

"You can wait here." Her fingers clutched tight to the banister. "I'm sure in the same house qualifies."

"You or the company of your charming sister?"

Anna couldn't miss the thick layer of sarcasm.

"Difficult." He stared up the curving flight of the back stairs. Anna clung to the warm banister, fighting the need to run her fingertips along that hard-angled jaw. "And I'm enjoying your charade." Steel blue eyes impacted hers. "The woman oppressed by her wicked older sister. Very...endearing."

"Yes, Zach, everything is a play for your benefit," Anna said, forcing her feet to climb the steep stairs.

What had she expected? That he would see the truth in the situation and side with her? That was stupid. She had lied to him for six long years, built a thick fog of deceit around her life.

"So you live in the attic apartment?"

Anna closed her eyes against the amusement in his voice. "Part of it."

"Even better." A soft chuckle sent heat flaring over her skin. "You're really going full tilt for the Cinderella angle. I'm impressed."

She stopped. Anger scalded the pit of her stomach. A smile cut her mouth. "Does this make you the other ugly sister?"

"Anna..." He shook his head, but his eyes sparked with sly humour. "I'm hurt. Surely, I'm Prince Charming."

"Hardly."

She turned on the second landing and began to climb the narrow stairs that led to her rooms. If nothing else, trawling up and down the stairs for all the years she had lived at Ashford had kept her fit.

"If I was at all dishonourable, I'd have to make a comment about your legs."

Anna ignored it. But she cursed the flush that rose through her face. She should be too old to blush. She really should...but she could almost feel his gaze raking over her skin. She took a steadying breath. Focus on something else. Yes. She had to get something out in the open. Her heart pounded. Maybe he wouldn't remember...

"The artist tonight is an old friend. Sofia wants to be a patron of the arts this month. So I thought someone who deserves it should benefit."

"You're the fairy godmother now?"

"Find this funny, Zach." She stopped on the small, low-ceilinged landing and fished in her bag for her keys. "But don't ruin tonight for Freddie."

"Lewis?"

Zach hung over her, too close in the confined space. His familiar scent wrapped around her and every measured breath touched her. Her skin prickled.

Anna closed her eyes. That tone. And she hadn't thought about it. Not really. Just believed that Zach wouldn't remember.

She was stupid. It was denial. Zach forgot nothing. Forgave nothing. She knew that all too well.

"Yes. Freddie Lewis." She pushed at the door.

"You're still in contact with him?"

Anna put her keys in a bowl on the side table. The cold glass was a relief against her tight fist. She hadn't found the courage to look at him. This was a part of the truth she couldn't tell him. If Zach learned the lies ran deeper still... No. Not going there.

She turned and the protective mask slid over her face. Anna gave him a short smile. "He's a friend from school." Her gaze dropped to focus on his tie. All of this was her fault...and Freddie had suffered. The stress she had put him under had sent his life into a fast downward spin. It was years, but the guilt still gnawed. "And he's had a hard time recently."

Zach pushed back the curtain to the narrow window before he looked at her. He was too tall in the low-ceiled room. Anna blinked. Zach in her room. Her skin started to itch.

"So I understand."

Anna wanted to thump him. Her hands curled into fists, nails digging into her palms. The sharp pain brought focus. He did this. Goaded her. "You don't have to sound so pleased about it."

"Nobody betrays me, Anna." The bedroom was suddenly too small, the walls pressing in on her senses. Her heartbeat thudded in her ears. "And you did."

"It's what you wanted."

"What I wanted? Really." He was so close she fought the urge to back away from him. In the small room, there was nowhere to go. "For a woman to throw me over for a scruffy boy?"

His pride was monumental. "Yes."

"Did he compare?"

"How dare—"

"Oh please, Anna, enough with the outraged virgin."

Incensed, she became reckless. "Of all men, *you* should know that I'm not."

A muscle jumped in his jaw. "No."

"Still *that* denial."

Anna turned to her wardrobe. Better to concentrate on clothes than rake up their disastrous past.

"You weren't a virgin, Anna."

Zach obviously had different ideas.

She stared, unseeing, at the neatly arranged rack of clothes. Her chest felt tight and more tears burned her eyes. She shouldn't have had wine at the lunch. Her and alcohol really didn't mix in the afternoon. But it wasn't just the drink. His words hurt. That he could dismiss her so easily. "Fine," she muttered. "Then I won't admit I'd never even kissed a man before that Christmas party."

His bark of harsh laughter made her jump. "That's stretching the truth, even for you."

Anna gripped tight to the image of the tumble-down house set in overgrown acres. It would be hers. Last the week, and it would be hers. She would be going home. "I thought you'd enjoy the idea." She looked back over her shoulder, found him in the doorway to her tiny kitchen. His eyes sparked fire. Stupid to antagonise this man. But something in her... Anna couldn't help herself. "Someone...untouched. Your wife told me—"

"*Ex*-wife." The word was a growl. "And she is not open to discussion."

Anna fixed her attention back on her clothes. Something looked different. "Didn't seem to bother her." Her voice was almost to herself. "Seemed more than happy to talk about you and your—"

"What?"

The edge of fury to his voice shot through her. Needling him. They had known each other too long, knew which buttons set off sparks. Anna's heart beat faster. Her lips dried. "Your...need to be the first."

"Is that what she said?"

"I thought we weren't discussing her?"

Anna's head felt light. He was closer, she knew, could *feel* him. She was playing with fire. Just the two of them in her bedroom. And there would be no one to interrupt. Sofia would still be drinking with her cronies. There would be no one to stop Anna giving into what her body craved—

Stupid thoughts. No.

Pick out a dress. Get ready. Get out.

"Your Cinderella image is slipping." His soft measured voice, always with the hint of dislike, was close, just behind her, but she would have to turn her head. No. Not doing that. Her dresses. Concentrate on them. Anna blinked. What...? These weren't her clothes.

She pulled off one hangar, then another.

Exclusive designer labels screamed expense. "Sofia."

"Oh I see, just more of the pantomime."

Anna ignored the hard sarcasm in his voice. She found more hangars, throwing them on to her nearby bed. Nothing of hers was left. Nothing. Just expensive...fripperies...following Sofia's dubious taste. Damn. Every single thing was clingy. Some moved into slut territory. Anna couldn't stop the blush that burned over her skin. She remembered Sofia wearing something exactly like it. The paparazzi had almost blinded them with flashes.

Zach picked up the gauzy, practically transparent dress. "So this is yours," he murmured. He glanced back at her. His expression was hard. Irritated. "Sofia borrowed it."

Yes. Everybody remembered that dress.

And he happily believed the worst of her. However, that was her own fault. It was something she'd fostered. But what was it to do with him anyway? The side of her Zach drew out spoke, "What d'you think?" She tugged the dress free from his tight grip, stared down at the transparent fabric against her clothes, moulding it to her frame. "Yes."

"No."

Anna bit down on her smile. Irritating him was...exciting. It had been so long since she'd been in his company. It was a forgotten emotion. "But it covers everything."

"No."

"The right accessories."

"No one is seeing you naked this week, Anna." He paused. "Except me."

Her head shot up, her face on fire, and found a cruel, mocking gleam to his eyes. She should call him a few very choice names...but her body thrummed at the thought, at the memory of his touch.

"No," she said.

"It's inevitable."

Anna's head jerked another no. Anger burned away the shock to her senses. "You are the most conceited... You seriously think, that after all that's happened I would...would jump into bed with you?"

That drew an infuriating curl to his mouth. "A bed. We never got to the bed, did we?"

Anna crushed her eyes against memories that had haunted her for years. The bitter fight searing into something neither of them had expected. No. That was another lie. "I have to get ready."

"Then you're wearing this."

Zach held something that was no more than a puddle of white silk in his hands.

"I don't need you to dress me, Zach."

An eyebrow lifted. The heat in his eyes made it difficult to breathe. "Someone needs to take you in hand."

Anna glanced back to the pile of clothes on the bed. All of them were awful. And this was Zach. Appearances were everything to him. She snatched the dress and marched into the bathroom. Shooting back the bolt, she spied the old key still in the lock. She twisted that too.

Anna stared at the dress, then draped it over her towel rail and buried her face in her hands. This was a nightmare. Her temples started to throb.

What the hell was she doing?

ഇൻ

Zach winced.

He hadn't missed the bolt *and* the lock.

A hand ran over his face, fingers scratching through his hair. "Coffee." He stared blankly at the cupboards. "I need coffee."

The kitchen was tiny and there was barely room to turn around. "This is beyond a joke." Water splashed into the kettle and he flicked the switch. "Everything for show."

He let out a slow breath.

Damn it. He shouldn't have brought up the past.

But the fact that she was still *friends* with Freddie Lewis swelled the old anger in his gut. "None of my business." Zach scrubbed at his face again. "Absolutely none of my business."

He rummaged through the cupboards and found instant. It would have to do. He needed something to smash through the stupid half-haze of alcohol. It had to be the drink dredging up images he had buried, memories of how she tasted, the incredible softness of her skin. And to keep pushing her when he could not have her—

His mug clattered onto the wooden countertop.

No.

This was a plan concocted by Anna and Sofia. They wanted the company his father and Gregory Brabant had built from the ground up. He would not allow two money-hungry harpies to destroy that effort, that legacy.

The coffee scalded his mouth and Zach grimaced.

"I hope you're laughing, Gregory. Because I am *not* amused." He glanced up at the kitchen clock. 6:20. He closed his eyes. The night stretched out before him. People milling about, balancing their wine and nibbles, the air thick with their endless, inane chatter.

More coffee burned its way down his throat.

And the knowledge that Anna would be there, taunting him, teasing him with no effort at all. A ball of anger tightened in his gut. Freddie Lewis. The man she had...hunted...after him. Anna had an itch she needed to scratch. He didn't want to believe the rumours...but he had firsthand evidence from that afternoon. Any man would do.

He drained the mug.

No. His ex-wife and Anna had taught him a lesson. He winced. A bitter one. It was why he set limits in his relationships. And he made very sure that a woman understood. He did not get involved. He never—

Zach stared.

Anna.

He hadn't even heard the shower. While he'd been burning his mouth on coffee, she'd been naked.

He crushed the images that scorched his mind. Crushed them. Hard.

Damp hair curled around her cheek, clung to her neck. Her skin glowed. The room filled with the soft scent of herbal soap and clean skin. A long, brown bathrobe reached past her knees. The thick material frayed at the edges and it hardly flattered her...but beneath he *knew* she was naked.

Zach's fingers tightened around the empty mug, still hot in his hand.

"What?" Angry brown eyes drilled him.

"It suits you." And that was the first idiotic thing that popped into his head. Her face, still warm and glistening from the shower, free of makeup... Reality slammed into his gut. He'd forgotten, been denying it. Anna was breathtaking.

"Though whether you should wear a dressing gown..."

He watched perfect lips purse.

"Funny." She rummaged through a drawer. A frown creased her forehead and her cheeks glowed. She finally stuffed something scrunched into her pocket. "I won't be long." She waved at his mug. "And you're obviously making yourself at home."

The gauche act wouldn't fool him. Not this time.

So he found her attractive. So what? He was a very rich man. Beautiful women swarmed around him. He wasn't Gregory, losing every sense over a woman nearly half his age. His jaw tightened. And he wasn't his father. Trapped by a scheming woman intent on enjoying his wealth.

Zach followed the slow slide of a droplet of water that slipped over her jaw, throat, clavicle and disappeared into the shadow of her skin.

Yes. His pride be damned.

He would enjoy Anna.

He held her gaze, saw the brief, fake flash of uncertainty, then the shine of something else.

Zach smiled. "Get dressed, Anna."

She blinked and then shot back into the bathroom.

Enjoy her and discard her.

As she had done to him.

But trust her? Never.

Chapter Six

"Stop looking at me like that."

The man had the infuriating cheek to look innocent. "Like what?"

"You're old enough. I shouldn't have to explain."

A smile twitched over his mouth and Anna knotted her hands. The desperate need to slap him had come back. The curve of those lips was an irritant that she couldn't ignore. Yes, either slap him...or kiss him. Shocked at that thought, Anna focused on the short run of stone steps which led into the gallery.

There was something different about Zach. It was annoying her that she couldn't work out what it was.

Glass doors slid open.

No. Not thinking about Zach.

Tonight was about Freddie.

Her clicking heels echoed through the white, vaulted entrance. A teak reception desk curved into one corner. Through another set of glass doors she could see the main gallery space. It looked empty. Where was—

"Anna! Thank God someone's here." Freddie wrapped her in a bear hug.

"Freddie." Her laughter was strained. Zach's gaze burned through her, his jaw tight. He stood back, silent. Disapproving.

Anna pulled free, stepping back from her friend, but still holding his hands. His grip was fierce. Her heart twisted. This had all been her fault. She met Freddie's familiar sharply handsome face and fixed a warm, reassuring smile to her mouth. "It will be fine. More than fine. You'll sell everything."

He stared about the empty space. "Who to?"

The doors whooshed open. "To them maybe." A group of four people, laughing and chatting, burst into the silent space. "Go." Anna gave his arm an affectionate shove. "Be charming. And sell them something."

"Anna. I love you." With that he was gone.

She couldn't look at Zach. Anger rippled off him. Anna focused on her heels clicking over the slate floor and keeping her steps even.

Her chest cramped, but she had to ignore it.

Zach only added to the stress of the evening. It didn't help that she could feel the light brush of his fingers at the base of her spine. She had to focus on something else. Freddie's words. A stupid thing for him to say...but that was who he was. She wouldn't deny him the excitement of the night. His life had been hard enough.

Anna put that from her mind and stared at the vivid rushes of blue on the huge canvas hanging before her. She knew nothing about art. She was trying to concentrate on the great sweep—

Zach's fingers, that soft, yet persistent pressure at the base of her spine, caressing the flow of silk against the bare skin beneath. A shiver ran through her body. Why was he still touching her? Being with her was the last thing he wanted. He had made that very clear.

101

"What are you doing, Zach?" Anna closed her eyes and fought the blush. Did her voice have to sound so...so...breathless?

His head dipped, so close she could feel the heat of his skin. His scent wove around her and she hated the way her stomach did that stupid little flip-flop of excitement.

"This is public." The brush of his warm breath over her ear forced Anna to hold back a second shiver. "Gregory wanted us to look public."

Her hands clenched into fists. "It isn't an 'us'," Anna muttered. "We're just to be seen together. Not seen *together*."

She felt his grin, the change in his breath over her skin. "And men would think me insane if I wasn't seen touching you."

Anna couldn't help it, her gaze snapped up to his. Sharp. Gleaming. She had to remember. Breathe in. Breathe out. "You...you chose this dress."

"I'm sure you meant me to."

His gaze scorched a path down her face. Delayed on her mouth in a way that made fire burn through her veins, but moved on, skimming the straight run of creamy white silk that clung to her skin and ended just above her knee. Anna knew she should be indignant. He wasn't surveying a piece of prized horseflesh—

That sharp gaze held her again. There was something hard in it. "It should've been conservative. But your nature shines through."

There was the familiar stone in her chest. "My nature?"

His finger traced a path down her bare arm and Anna couldn't stop the prickling of her skin. "Freddie still loves you, does he?"

Anna stepped back, moving beyond his touch. Cold washed through her after the heat of his fingertips. "It's an expression, Zach. He says it to everyone."

"Do you?"

"What? Say it to everyone?" There was the lie she could tell him. That of course she told each man she met of her undying love. Zach would see her as the trivial airhead who had kept him away from her. But she had made a promise to herself. A new life. One without lies. She just had to ignore the tension tightening her neck. "No. I don't." But she wouldn't add that she'd never said it to anyone. That truth, like so many others, was too raw to speak.

"No. Do you love him?"

Anna blinked. Damn. She couldn't admit that Freddie been in on her little charade so many years ago. That he had helped her. She couldn't let him think any worse of Freddie. She didn't want to imagine the damage Zach could do to him.

"As a friend."

Zach's lip curled. "Turn out he wasn't rich enough for you?"

Her insides twisted. Zach and his money. "So you think he's a poor prospect for me?"

"He should be grateful he is." Zach's gaze drilled her. Darkened, cut with silver.

Anger roiled though her gut and she had the desperate need to wipe that smug smile from his mouth. Nails dug into her palms. But the pain didn't distract her. It couldn't. "He's more of a man than you—"

His sudden flash of fury killed her words.

Stupid thing to for her to say. She should know better than to antagonise him. But she really couldn't help herself.

"Is that what you think?" His voice, cool, dangerous. Anna wasn't calling the sudden heat through her body panic. She wasn't. Her attention shot to the door. Freddie was still chatting, arms waving, charming new patrons. It was a public place. Zach wouldn't risk his reputation here, now. "Have you no memory, Anna? Can't you remember when you last wore a dress like this?"

The honeyed caress of his words stole over her skin. She fought to breathe, not to sink into the soft warmth of them. Zach was playing his games. Always. She forced a glare. "I try not to think about it." Good. Strong, clear voice. Steady.

"Try?"

She followed his movements, willing the panic to calm. They were in a public place. The Christmas party had been too. No, this was *more* public.

Where was he going?

Anna hissed out a breath. His warm fingers, then palms, slipped over her shoulders, cupped them. The solid build of his body shielded her. And his lips, brushing the shell of her ear.

"How hard do you have to try to keep me out of your mind, Anna?"

She swallowed back in a parched mouth. Her nervous tongue touched her lips. She felt his satisfied smile. Damn him. "It's no effort at all, Zach."

"Really?"

She closed her eyes against the lick of that word, the promise it held. "Really."

"Then this should be just as easy to forget."

His warm mouth slid over her neck...and then the nip of his teeth teased her earlobe. Anna gasped, tried to pull away, but his hands shaped down her body, pressing her against him.

Butterfly kisses stole over her neck, quick, pulsing. Fire pooled swift, low in her belly and she couldn't help herself. Her neck curved, offering him more skin to touch, to taste.

The slow run of his hands over silk thrummed Anna's skin, every inch of her aware, aware of him.

This is what he did to her, made her wanton, desperate for him.

She didn't care. Didn't care that they were in the middle of a gallery, that anyone could see them. She couldn't stop.

His long, clever finger found her through the silk and a soft, breathy moan escaped her.

"Zach. We shouldn't."

"Old times, Anna." His mouth lingered on her shoulder. "This dress, the dark, and us."

Another finger joined the first, circling, the silk slipping over her skin in smooth, slow ripples. It pulsed a hot ache through her. Her head fell back against the strength of his shoulder and her throat dried.

"Remember me now, Anna?"

She swallowed. "Yes. But we really should..."

His other hand pushed down over her hip and more fingers rubbed and touched and... Little flashes of light burst behind her eyelids.

"Should what, Anna?" His roughened breath brushed her ear and the heat in her body soared, flared. "Should I stop? I think I—"

"No!" Her hands gripped his. He couldn't stop. Not now.

Oh, God. Please.

Not—

The orgasm splintered her.

A wave of heat washed through her trembling body. Anna bit her lip, caging the desperate need to cry out, to shout Zach's name, declare—

The creak of a glass door.

Oh God...

He had just...in the middle of a gallery. Anyone, anyone, could have seen them. Shame swam through her, but her legs were still too shaky to stand without help. The solid strength of Zach's body held her up. She hated and craved it. The slow, slow slide of his hands away from her left her cold. "Yes, you remember me now, Anna."

The edge of bitterness to his voice crushed her. She had just shown she was a complete... Anna shied away from the word. This was how she reacted to him. How she would always react to him. It didn't seem to matter how hard she fought it, her body was a traitor.

"Vaguely." Anna stepped away, straightened her dress with shaking fingers. She couldn't meet his gaze, fixing her attention on his tie. Heat still burned over her skin. "And what did that prove, Zach?"

He lifted her chin, forced her to meet his eyes. Fire burned there. "That this is far from over."

"I—"

"What have you been saying to my sister? She's practically scarlet." Sofia glanced over her silk dress. A cold smile curved her painted lips. "Anna. White? Daring of you."

Her sister was the last thing she needed. Zach had just... No. She couldn't think about it. Her mind was still fuzzy, her body not entirely her own. But she had to focus. Deal with Sofia's usual snide remarks. "You took all of my clothes."

"No." Her gaze slid away, searched the empty space of the gallery. Her lips still held the twist of her smile. "Actually I burned them."

The sudden need to cry surged through Anna. Another one of Sofia's callous little acts that had plagued her life for years. No. At the end of the week, it would be over. She reminded herself that they were just clothes. Comfortable, well-worn and easily replaceable.

She straightened and enjoyed the touch of a real smile on her mouth. "Good. Thank you."

Sofia's smile froze, for just a fraction of a second. It widened Anna's own smile and gave her a sense of power. Sharp eyes narrowed on Anna. "Have you organised *anything* tonight? I'm parched." Sofia stalked away to her cronies in the far corner, expensive heels clacking on the slate floor.

Anna let out a slow breath. Finally, *finally*, she had bested her sister.

"More of your little show?"

But there was still Zach. And what they had just done.

Anna knew she should feel ashamed. Knew it. But that little quiver held her, the thrill of danger, of them being caught. Her blood hummed with it. And it shouldn't. "I've said it before, Zach. I'll leave you to think what you will." Her gaze flicked over his, but she couldn't hold it. "I need to see to the caterers."

"Always at your sister's whim."

"No." Anna straightened. "This is for Freddie. I owe him."

She turned away, her heart thudding. A new life. One without the complication of Zach. Anna made herself breathe. That wasn't the raw burn of emotion in the pit of her stomach...no...despite all that food, she was hungry again. That was all. Feelings for a man like Zach?

With all that she had seen, all that she knew?

Her insides soured.

Anna grimaced. Damn. Now she had heartburn.

ℬℭ

"Aren't you going to introduce us?" A slight smile touched his mother's mouth.

Somehow Maria Quinn didn't look any older, still the pale beauty who had caught his father so many years before. A knot twisted in his back.

"She's busy," he said.

Zach stopped himself from grinding his teeth. Which one of them had invited his mother to this show? Had to be Sofia. Anna's manoeuvrings were never so...brash. He took another glass from a passing waiter. This day couldn't be over soon enough.

Change the subject, far away from Anna Shrewsbury. "So... How are you?"

"Fine." She twisted the glass of sparkling water she held. "How was the lunch?"

She looked up and Zach found himself meeting his own eyes. It had to be the lights. That wasn't the sheen of tears. "The usual." Zach couldn't hold her gaze, torn with the reality that she had never been invited. "But not a substitute for having him here."

A small sigh escaped her. "No." She paused. "I was sorry to hear about Gregory. I know the two of you were close." Maria's gaze rested on Sofia, laughing and shouting at a waiter for more champagne. "She seems to be taking it well."

Zach forced down the smile. They also shared the same sense of humour.

"Zach..."

Damn, another attempt to explain, to win him over. "Mother—"

"She's different."

He stared. "What?"

"Your woman in white. She's not your usual perfect plastic doll." Her eyes narrowed. "Who is she?"

Zach expelled a slow breath. Let his mother laugh at him now. He was out with a gold digger, when he had vowed— "Anna Shrewsbury."

"Ah, Sofia's sister." Maria's smile widened and she patted his arm. Long, pale fingers stayed. "Good."

He stared at her hand and the years he hadn't spoken, hadn't seen her, weighed heavy. But he couldn't forget what she had done. She claimed she had always loved his father, but the whole world had known of her affairs. "Good? You know her reputation?"

"And it's not bothering you." Her smile deepened. "Are you starting to mellow in your old age?" A cool hand framed his jaw for a brief second. "I loved your father—"

"You betrayed him."

"I *loved* your father. Still do. And he loved me. We didn't marry for money or convenience. I..." she looked away, "...strayed. I'm not proud of it. But it's something I have to live with. Something he forgave." Maria took a sip of her water. "Your Anna..."

Zach automatically found her in the crowd, caught in a shot of light. His gut tightened in the all-too-familiar way. Did she have to flirt with that old walrus?

109

"...isn't perfect. You can't control what she'll do. Or who she'll do it with."

Zach could hardly contain his disbelief. "And you see *that* as being a step forward?"

Sharp blue eyes held his. "For you? Yes."

And then Zach had to watch her leave, passing one of the gallery assistants pressing another red dot on to the frame of yet another painting. Yes. There was a reason why he hadn't talked to his mother for twelve years.

He scrubbed a hand over his face.

Damn it. Think of something else. He caught that old moustachioed walrus kissing Anna's hand and her delicate responding blush. No, something *else*. The assistant with her little red dots. Freddie Lewis was having a successful evening. Grudgingly, Zach had to admit that he deserved it.

He stared into the dark red depths of his wine. Guilt gnawed at him. His mother's words. Saying that his father had forgiven her... But she was wrong about one thing. He would find control with Anna. Purge himself of the insane desire to push her up against the nearest wall.

As he had six years ago.

But then six years ago, he'd lashed out. Disgusted at himself for succumbing to Anna's wiles, he then caught her with another man. She was engaged to him within the week. Sharp light cut over the smooth surface of his wine. He could still feel the burn of rage, how his hands had balled into fists and he had wanted to pound some sense into Freddie. Anyone involving themselves with one of the Shrewsbury sisters needed to be warned.

Zach let out a slow hot breath.

Freddie Lewis was there now, snatching a quiet moment before he had to charm more people into buying his work. Anna was beyond his forgiveness. But him?

Zach found himself walking towards the younger man. "Freddie."

Eyes as dark as Anna's narrowed on him. "I thought it was you." The younger man straightened, put his empty wineglass on a convenient table. "Still hounding Anna?"

Zach couldn't help the smile. Yes, Anna was already weaving her lies. "Is that what she told you?" He searched the noisy crowd of people, but no flash of white silk stood out. Where was walrus...? No. Zach put *that* from his mind. He turned back to Freddie. His smile faded. "I did what I did as a warning. Believe it or not, I was trying to protect you."

A short bark of laughter stopped his words. "Protect me? You ruined my career."

Zach ignored him, cutting through his protest. "But that's in the past. Now." He paused, waiting for Freddie to calm himself. The belligerent gleam faded. Good. He wasn't a fool. "I like your work. And I can offer you a commission."

"Is this your attempt to make amends?"

"No."

Freddie blinked.

"It's not a sinecure, Freddie. Contact Elise Michaels, my PA. Make an appointment." From the corner of his eye, he caught Anna. Her face was flushed and worry edged her eyes. It was obvious Freddie hadn't told Anna what Zach had done. Was it Freddie's own pride keeping him silent? "This is business. Again, it has nothing to do with her."

"Hurt Anna and I don't care how rich you are," Freddie said. "This time I will stop you."

Zach stared at him. "What—"

"Everything's started to wind down." Anna's smile was too wide, she could feel it, but she had to interrupt. Zach and Freddie couldn't talk. Her old friend had transformed into the overprotective brother once too often. Anna couldn't see him jeopardise his career. Not now. "I just managed to escape old Sir Nigel... And I think you sold every last thing."

"Looks that way." Freddie paused. "How are you getting home, Anna?"

And there he went. "I'm fine." She tucked a lock of her hair behind her ear and her gaze dropped briefly. She couldn't help it. Embarrassment had her panicked. "Zach's taking...giving me a lift."

"Call me when you get in."

"Freddie..."

"Anna..."

"All right." She caught the gallery owner waving and pointing. "I think Adam wants to talk to you."

Freddie kissed her cheek. He stabbed a finger at her. "The minute you get in."

Anna watched him leave.

"You've been avoiding me," Zach murmured.

"What did you say to Freddie?"

The ghost of a smile touched his mouth and Anna felt the fire of all–too-familiar anger shoot through her veins. "What did you think I said?"

"I'm not playing your games, Zach!"

Two women turned and stared. Anna twitched a smile at them and took a calming breath. Her voice dropped to a rushed whisper. "Your problem is with me, not with him."

"This loyalty is...unexpected."

A warm hand slid over her elbow. Air hissed from her lungs at the contact. Anna had thrown herself into the organisation, the administration that still needed her oversight. She hadn't thought about Zach. She hadn't— "What are you doing?"

"Don't worry, Anna. Nothing quite so public this time."

The undercurrent of laughter to his voice irked her. She should have stopped him. She could have. Anna couldn't deny the truth. She craved anything Zach deigned to give her. Her lust for him was blatant. Anna hated herself for wanting him. And damn the man, it wasn't amusing. "You surprise me." Good. Her voice was cool. In all too short a time, she wouldn't have to think about Zach at all. And she would never make the mistake of revealing how much she craved him. "Isn't public what you wanted?"

Fingers tightened around her elbow. Zach urged her forward. "Funny."

"Excuse me." Anna tried to pull her arm free and failed. Not making a scene, not making a scene. "What... Where are we going?"

"Home."

"H—" She couldn't say the word. Anna swallowed back in a dry throat. "Home?" Damn, now it sounded strangled.

"That was the deal too." His eyes fixed on her. "Though if I remember correctly, the sleeping arrangements were at our own discretion."

"I'm not... Before..." Her hands flapped. "That...that was a mistake."

He answered with a predatory smile. "As was Petersen's office, the bar, *my* office, the car, the kitchen..."

Zach acknowledged the gallery owner and Freddie. Her friend's face darkened, his mouth thinning. Anna's smile was bright, deliberately so. She mimed phoning him and got a brief nod.

The inner glass door slid silently shut behind them.

"I've told you, what's going to happen is inevitable."

This time Anna yanked her arm free. "Why you arrogant—"

Zach placed a finger against her lips. Anna froze. "Sh-h-h," he murmured, the soft low tone licking her senses.

A spotlight cast deep shadow over his face and the memory of Carl's office washed over her. Those insane little kisses. Her breath hitched.

"We can add an unofficial codicil to Gregory's will." His finger traced her lips then followed the plane of her jaw. Eyes gleamed with bright fire. "Do you agree?"

"Zach, this is insane..."

"No. We need this." He paused. "Stay with me..."

Anna's heart squeezed tight, so tight she gasped. "Stay—"

"...with no strings, no promises, no stupid ideas." He smiled. "That's not who we are." He let out a slow breath. "After the week, we walk away. And whatever this is will be sated."

Anna closed her eyes.

She thought the years of Sofia's snide little remarks had inured her to simple words bringing pain. After the soaring elation now came the bitter truth. Sex. Used for sex and discarded, like any other of his long line of women. What had she thought he would say?

Stay with me...

Her own joy mocked her.

...I need you, I care—

She snorted at that ridiculous thought. The last man to care about her, to care about anyone was Zach. He'd already proven that. And caring about her was the last thing she wanted from him.

"No." Anna shook her head. It was just her limited experience that demanded she say yes. Nothing more. She was making a break from her old life. Playing Zach's games belonged to her past. "That would be...unwise."

"Unwise?"

She found his narrowed gaze focused on her. A muscle jumped in his jaw. Great. Now he was insulted. "This is hardly the place, Zach."

His features tightened. "I don't—"

The click of heels behind them interrupted him. "Going so soon?"

Sofia's sharp voice cut across Anna. She winced. "It's half past eleven, Sofia."

"As I said, early." She smirked and her gaze slid over Zach in a way that made Anna's skin crawl. "Well have fun...I know I would."

"I'll never know what Gregory saw in you." His words were almost a growl.

Sofia's smile grew. "You never wanted to find out, Zach. I was too much of a woman for you." She turned away, patting Anna's bare shoulder. "Stick with my sister. She can't begin to compare."

"No. She doesn't," Zach said.

Sofia stopped. "I'm surprised," she muttered. "And you so rarely do that, Anna." The smile curved her bright red lips again, hard. It didn't touch her gleaming eyes. "Just make sure to burn him like you do all the others." Her hand flicked a wave. "Night."

"Your sister is always..." Zach frowned. Disgust thinned his mouth.

"Yes."

Anna wanted to climb into bed, pull the covers over her head and sleep. Maybe wake up and discover that the whole of the previous day had been some bizarre nightmare.

"So, Anna, you've refused me. Again."

Zach and his inability to drop a difficult subject. Another thing she really hated about him. "Not here." Anna forced her feet forward. She was caught, trapped. Anna could almost taste the freedom that the next week would bring...but first she had to deny Zach what he wanted. The small, persistent thought stung. What they both wanted.

The chauffeur stood beside the open door of the sleek, black Bentley.

Chilled air swept around her and she shivered. At least she told herself it was the coolness of the night and not the slide of Zach's warm fingers over her arm. Anna pulled at the seat belt and closed her eyes. His scent wove through her senses.

Her stomach cramped with nerves. And with something else.

But to say yes...

To spend the week with him.

Her throat tightened. No. It was insane even to think it.

Anna caught his profile, sharp, beautiful. She had lusted after this man for six years. In that moment, Anna knew a week would never be enough.

Chapter Seven

What was she doing here?

Anna watched the car pull away from the kerb and disappear into the night. There were butterflies in her stomach. It was too much like *that* night.

Standing on the pavement outside of the exclusive mansion block, nerves eating her as she rubbed her fingers again and again over stolen keys—

"Come on, Anna."

Zach's hand on her arm jolted her out of her memory. Yes. Best not to dwell on those events and the reason behind them. She had been a stupid girl of nineteen with a head full of romantic rubbish.

The uniformed doorman opened the outer doors, carefully avoiding looking at her. He was not the same man who had let her in years before, knowing that she was an in-law to Gregory Brabant. Instead, he gave Zach a brief nod and murmured, "Mr. Quinn."

Golden lamplight washed over the opulent entrance hall. The familiar scent of lemon polish, the hint of leather from the armchairs shot her mind back. Panic hit her. "I can stay in a hotel, Zach. I won't tell—"

"Of course you would," he said, his fingers growing firm around her arm. "The second I let you walk out of those doors, you'd be on the phone to Petersen."

It hurt that he thought so little of her. "Honestly, Zach—"

His bark of laughter cut her off. "Honest? You?" He gave a short acknowledgment to the man at the desk and then Zach stabbed at the lift button. "Even my mother's heard of your reputation."

Anna blinked. "Your mother?"

"As if you didn't know. But she's cut from the same cloth as you. An unhealthy obsession with money and men." The lift pinged and wooden doors creaked back. Zach urged her forward. "And not necessarily in that order."

Anna had a vague memory of a tall, blonde woman, delicate, incredibly beautiful. She remembered Gregory telling her that Zach's parents had been devoted to each other. "Gregory said—"

"Yes. I know." There was a bitter turn to his voice. He dropped her bag and pressed the button for the top floor. "Hardly the best judge of relationships, was he?"

Anna's heart thudded. Her memory was as sharp as if their first disastrous encounter had happened only hours before. A nervous glance found Zach's face. His jaw was tight, his attention focused on the floor dial. Was he starting to remember?

It was insane.

She had confused lust and infatuation with something else...and in a rush of youth had decided to act upon it. With disastrous consequences. It was a lesson she had to keep close. Zach had already made one dangerous offer, one she still wanted to accept.

The lift creaked and the doors slid open.

"You know the way."

Silver-edged eyes held her and Anna couldn't breathe. Heat flushed her face. She fought down another burst of memory. And failed.

Silently opening the main door to his penthouse apartment, tiptoeing through the dark hall and finding Zach standing before the great bay window of the drawing room. A single lamp splashed light. He had obviously come back late from the office, thrown off his jacket, half rolled his sleeves and grabbed a drink. Formally dressed, he was beautiful. Casual, he was devastating. And her gaze devoured him.

He downed the rest of his whiskey and grimaced.

Anna found her courage and swallowed back in a dry throat. "Zach…"

The empty tumbler hit the deep rug.

"Anna? What the hell are you doing here? Get out. Now."

"Yes. I know the way."

Her heels sank into the deep carpet. God, it felt like a walk to the gallows.

The silence. Just the soft tread of feet and breathing. Anna tried to keep her own measured, controlled. Involving herself with Zach would be madness. Her hands knotted. Utter and complete madness.

The doors opened on to the wide hall. Zach waited for her to precede him…but her heart was hammering and her mouth was dry. The place still looked the same. Smooth pale walls stretching up into high, beautifully corniced ceilings. Dark walnut floors. Paintings, simple and priceless. She had always loved Zach's apartment. It oozed elegance. Just like its owner.

"Anna. I told you. I can contain myself."

"Really?" She'd heard the dark humour in his voice. She had to get a grip. She wasn't an awestruck teenager anymore. "I've seen little evidence of it."

An eyebrow lifted. His eyes sparked. "You have no idea."

Her heart squeezed. "Zach—"

"Are you hungry?" He dropped her bag beside the hall table and turned to the kitchen. "Go. Sit. I'll be through in a minute."

The drawing room.

"Just a room," Anna muttered under her breath. "That's all it is."

She forced her feet through the open doors and into that too familiar space. She flicked on a switch, casting a pale light over the dining table. It was enough. More than enough. She knew this room, had visited it in dreams, in waking thoughts so many times. The same dark floors and pale walls. Sleek white furniture...

"How did you get in?"

Zach stalked towards her, anger twisting his features. She didn't know this man, she didn't... Anna tried to open her mouth. But she only found herself stumbling backwards, trying to evade his fury.

"Keys?" Zach snatched them from her hands, turning them over in the bright wash of light from the table lamp.

"These are Gregory's." Sharp eyes narrowed on her. "What do you think you're doing here, Anna?"

"I—"

Stupid. She felt so stupid. She had been certain. Certain that he wanted something more from her than a casual fumble. The way he had looked at her, kissed her. Touched her. Her throat tightened and she fought the burn of tears. Her spine hit cool plaster. Was Isabelle right, after all? That Zach was a player?

That he really couldn't help trying to seduce every woman he met?

She straightened, held the fury directed at her. Yes. And she'd be damned if he thought she was looking for him. "I thought you were out of town."

His sharp gaze slid over the ridiculously short dress and then returned to her face. Something glittered there. "And you thought to use my apartment?" An edge to his voice sent a shiver over her skin.

He'd taken the lie. Anna's insides were a knot of nerves. She jerked a nod. "Yes."

Closer now. She sucked in his scent with every breath. Her head felt light.

"Use my bed?"

An unexpected pulse throbbed low in her belly. Anna could hardly breathe. Her heart pounded. So close now she could almost taste him. She swallowed. Continue the lie. "Yes."

A low growl made her gasp. "Over my dead body."

And then his mouth took hers and Anna forgot everything, everything *else.*

Her attention shot to *that* wall...and found a large cabinet obscuring it. Anna closed her eyes. Trembling fingers touched her lips. Yes. Hide it.

"Here." Plates slid onto the glass dining table. "There's not much. I wasn't expecting to entertain."

Anna stared at the plate of toast, thick with butter. She really didn't feel hungry. But she sat and poured water into a tall glass. Everything felt...off. She was sitting with Zach as if nothing had ever happened between them...but her skin still itched. She sipped at the water, letting it slide cold down her throat. She was tired, weary down to the bone. And she had to ask the question. "So..." Her words dried.

Zach stared at her. The hard gleam she found there made her heart patter. She blinked and turned her attention briefly to her glass. "Which bedroom is mine?"

A smile curved his mouth, predatory and just so...Zach. "Which one do you want?"

He never stopped. Just the relentless baiting as he tried to annoy her. And succeeded. "The one furthest away from you."

Zach lifted his glass. "I'm wounded." He gave her another slow smile. "But it will be an interesting test to see how long you can resist me"

"Could your ego be any bigger?"

"Am I wrong?"

"Yes."

"Ah-h, now it's become a matter of pride."

"And what's that supposed to mean?" Anna wanted to sink into a soft bed, pull cool sheets over her head and find sleep. But what she needed? That was something entirely different.

Zach pushed himself all too slowly out of his chair, his gaze never leaving hers.

Anna doubted she could stand.

Her legs ran liquid and a tremor pulsed through her frame. Run. She should run. Find a bedroom. Lock the door. Barricade it with furniture. All day, it'd been proven over and over that her body still ached for him. But he couldn't be part of her new life.

Steel blue eyes speared her.

He couldn't.

Zach belonged to her past.

Her lips were dry, throbbing. Anna felt every breath. His hand...closer, stroking over her hair, so gentle a caress she almost moaned. Their relationship was fire and anger. Not this. Not tenderness.

A thumb lifted her chin.

His face, shadowed, unknown. "Come with me, Anna."

The dark promise in his voice stole over her senses...and for a moment, an endless moment, her resolve wavered. The heat of his skin against hers. Losing herself in the arms of a man who had tormented her thoughts for years. But afterwards...

"After next week, we'll never see each other again."

His twist of a smile cut through the shadow. "Perfect."

It was so easy for him. Vainly, Anna wished she were the woman he thought she was. Then she could've happily spent the week in bed with him and not give leaving a second thought. But she wasn't that woman and she never would be. "I need to phone Freddie."

Zach's hand dropped away and cold steel glared at her. He stood back. "Your precious Freddie."

The stupid thought hit her that Zach was jealous. It faded just as quickly. She ignored the pain at its passing. No. That wasn't Zach. He thought too much of himself to think about anyone else. "You've never liked the idea of something you want focused on someone else."

A wry smile pulled at his mouth. "I'm sure he didn't compare."

Anna knew her face was red. She pushed herself out of her chair. Find her bag. Find her phone. He hadn't believed the truth but she had no intention of feeding his already bloated ego. "A lady doesn't tell."

"Lady."

There was that hint of derision again. The knot in Anna's gut tugged tight. Cool eyes slid to his. "That didn't seem to be bothering you a moment ago."

"Around you, my higher brain functions take a back seat."

That barb wounded. "My bag," she muttered and made for the hall.

Zach cursed. *What the hell did I say that for?* He watched Anna snatch up her bag and disappear into the study. There had been a flicker of hurt in her face. It stabbed him with guilt. He ran his hands through his hair and expelled a hot slow breath. "I said it because it's true." His laugh was bitter. "And I'm *so* smooth." He covered his eyes. "She always, *always* does this to me."

Zach knew what it was. Had always known.

The fury, the goading. It was foreplay. And it was driving him crazy.

He glanced at the clock. Far past midnight. Anna could have the bedroom next to the study, the furthest one from his. That was the sensible and safest thing to do. He had to forget about sleeping with her. She had, after all, turned him down. Twice.

He straightened, absently pulling at his tie. "Yeah. I should take the hint."

He snapped open shirt buttons. What he had done in the gallery. Only Anna could drive him to that insanity. The vanilla scent of her skin, the wet slide of silk—

Zach cursed. "No."

Damn the woman, she was doing this deliberately. Teasing him.

He was not going to fall for it this time.

Why couldn't she have been sensible and just accepted his offer? They could be—

He rapped on the study door. Hard.

"Anna?"

Anna pulled the phone away from her ear, wincing as Freddie's lecture continued. "Freddie…" Another rapid knock jolted through her frame. She stuck her phone on her ear again, staring down at the uncluttered desk that took up the small room. "Look. I'll explain everything—"

"Will you?" Zach's soft growl.

She stared at him, her heart in her throat. She hadn't heard the door. Damn. And what she had just said… "—next week." The words stumbled out. "I'll explain next week. Bye." She stabbed at the end-call button and switched the mobile off.

"I'll have that, thank you." Before she could react, he took the phone from her lax grip. "Can't leave you for a minute, can I, Anna?"

Damn the man. "You won't even let me have a private conversation now?" She straightened, met his hard gaze. "And I'll have that back."

A smile cut his mouth and the sudden gleam in his eyes made her heart rate jump. "Take it."

He slid the mobile into his trouser pocket.

Anna realised she was staring. She blinked and felt the anger surge. It was anger, that sudden rush of heat through her blood. "You're…disgusting."

"Really?"

Her thighs hit the desk. Anna started. She had hardly been aware she was moving, that Zach had backed her up. He was

125

still an arm's length away. Good. She wanted him to stay right there. "I'm not playing your game, Zach."

"No. You're playing one of your own."

He traced down her cheek and all breath stopped. "Zach..."

"I came in here to say good night. To leave you to sleep by yourself." His fingertip, slipping, sliding over her jaw, her throat, along the exposed length of her clavicle. His hot eyes burned into hers. Anna's skin was on fire. Her fingers clung to the edge of the desk, keeping her steady and stopping her own hands from stealing across the heat of his chest. "But you've made it obvious that you can't be left on your own. Not even for a second."

He followed the curve of her breast, focusing on her mouth. A sudden throb low in her belly made her gasp with the delicious reminder of where he could take her. A dangerous smile curved his mouth.

"It's been hours since I tasted you, Anna." His gaze scorched over her face, until his eyes found her again. Dark. Hungry. "And I did warn you. There would be penalties for misbehaving."

"I..." Words dried.

Closer. The heat of his body washed over her. His intoxicating scent. So close. His hand stroked over her breast, a clever, clever thumb finding the nipple—

Her mouth on his.

Not thinking.

Anna was *not* thinking.

Hot. The lingering taste of the *L'Evangile*, of its blackberries, raspberries...and the taste of him. Something that made her arms curl around his neck, fingers tight into his hair and drive his mouth hard against hers.

And then his hands, sliding rough over silk, lifting her, settling her on his desk and pressing hard.

Anna groaned. "Is that my mobile?"

Fierce eyes, edged with a dark humour gripped her. "No." His hips moved. "I should be insulted."

"I wouldn't—"

His lips slid along her jaw, found the intricate shell of her ear. Talking was overrated. Her hands stroked their way down his spine, the strong muscle of his back. It was wrong to let herself succumb to this need. To lose herself in this man again. *Once.* It was the whisper in her head. It pulsed with Zach's open-mouthed kisses over her throat, the curve of her bared shoulder. *Just once. To know him. Not a rushed fumble. Not to regret...*

"Zach."

He froze. Muscles tensed under her fingers. "Don't say it, Anna."

A smile lifted her mouth. This was her choice. This was freedom. "Pick a bedroom."

Chapter Eight

Zach stared at her. Stared until Anna felt an embarrassed flush rise over her skin. "What?"

"You're serious?"

"Yes."

He gave her a smile she felt all the way to her toes. His warm hand curved around her cheek, stroked over her skin. "I..."

Anna's gut tightened. "Don't say anything, Zach." Her gaze dropped away. He would make an offer, offer money, offer the strict role of his usual women. No. He couldn't spoil the moment with that. Her choice was free. To satisfy the itch. Yes. After Freddie, he had lashed those words at her.

"Anna?" Was that hesitation in his voice? He lifted her chin. Surprised, she found concern in his face. She blinked. "I'm sorry. You don't have to... If you don't..."

She fought down the warmth, the need to hold him and whisper something he could never hear. "This, we are inevitable, Zach." She slid off the desk and took his hand. Her fingers curled into its warmth and she tugged him forward. The mask slipped into place. "And I've always wanted to see your bed."

His hand tightened. The shine in his silvered eyes made her heart skip. No. Those thoughts didn't belong.

"It'll be my pleasure to show you."

Yes.

She couldn't start a new life with no regrets.

She squashed the other little voice that was screaming at her. Wanting her to be safe, to be sensible. To involve herself with Zach would only bring heartache.

No. It couldn't.

Her heart wasn't involved.

She had lusted after him for years, that she couldn't deny. But she didn't even *like* him. And she could hardly...hardly...that...with a man she didn't even like. A smile curled around her mouth. She had broken away from Sofia. This was her way of breaking away from Zach. It would be over and the rest of the week wouldn't have the fire and fury of that day.

There, quibbling, cautious voice. Argue with that.

"Anna?" Zach's voice was a delicious slide over her skin, breaking into stupid thoughts. "You're absolutely sure?"

Her mouth flattened. "I can make a decision by myself, Zach."

"You just looked..."

"What?"

A muscle jumped in his jaw and it flared heat through Anna's body. Lamplight angled his face. Memory of their first time swamped her, of how she had lost herself in him. She traced down his shirt, catching, flicking on the buttons. Her fingertips grazed the warmth of his skin and Anna sucked in a breath.

"You...wanted to see the bed."

She hadn't imagined the hesitation in his voice, had felt it through tensing muscles.

"Yes." Her smile felt wanton. "That and more."

"Then we're wasting time." His large, warm hand closed over hers and eased it into his own. There was just the short walk along the dimly lit hallway. Her shoes clicked against the dark walnut floor, but all she could focus on was her own uneven breathing.

She was growing more nervous by the second.

She should have stayed in the study, not stopped the rush of fire and passion that would have overwhelmed them. Her insides knotted. She hadn't wanted that. Anna wanted the luxury of a bed, to experience the ecstasy of naked skin.

Zach opened the door at the far end of the wall and stood back.

Anna's feet sank into deep pale carpet. Without thinking, she pulled her sandals free and let her bare toes curl into the softness. She sighed with relief and then her gaze skirted the room. Three huge floor-to-ceiling windows were shuttered against the night. A door led to a dressing room and she spied a bathroom beyond that.

And there was the bed.

Warm hands cupped her shoulders and she jumped.

"I do enjoy the fact that you're playing gauche to the bitter end."

His fingers slipped over her skin, found the concealed zip. Anna closed her eyes. The slide of his fingertips down her bared spine, a tender and teasing caress.

"Such incredible skin, Anna."

The murmur of his voice over her ear tickled her with his hot breath and she bit back a moan. Slowly, all too slowly, he eased the silk from her skin until it dropped to a puddle of cloth at her feet. Her arms, hands shot up to cover her nakedness.

"Oh no," Zach said softly. "I've never had the chance to truly appreciate you." His hands caressed her arms, a gentle persuasion. "Turn around."

"I..."

This wasn't exactly what she had imagined. Zach being naked had definitely been a high priority. But he was still *very* clothed.

"Anna..."

His voice was a drop of pure heat through her blood. A slow sigh escaped her. Anything, anything to have that voice, that mouth whispering over her skin. She turned.

Zach's look scorched down her body and Anna's blood pounded. Embarrassment gave way to something else. To a delight, a satisfaction in Zach wanting what he saw. And he did. Blazing eyes found her, dilated almost black.

His large hand framed her jaw, a thumb stroking over her lip.

Without thinking, her tongue darted, caught his thumb tip. He hissed.

She twitched a smile. "Aren't you going to return the favour?"

Zach's attention returned to his clothes, the half-open shirt. A sly smile cut his mouth. "I might... What can you trade me?"

Anna blinked. Should have known it wouldn't be simple with Zach. His amount of experience— No. She wasn't thinking about the number of women he had taken to his bed since their brief fling.

Her arms covered her breasts again.

"So there are rules." Zach stepped back and slow, practiced fingers slid over the buttons of his shirt. "As this is an *unofficial* agreement."

Anna's mouth ran dry. She couldn't help herself and stared at the expanse of brown, muscled flesh that came into her view with each slip of his fingers. He tugged the shirt free of his trousers and shrugged out of it.

Her body pulsed.

The sly smile still cut his mouth, his eyes searing her.

"What are your rules, Anna?"

She swallowed and found her voice. "This is a game-free zone, Zach."

"Now that *is* a pity."

She blinked. Every ounce of her inexperience weighed on her. Really? What was she doing? She glanced involuntarily over the smooth run of Zach's stomach muscles and with it came the urge to lick, to sink her teeth... She couldn't stop the smile.

A new life with no regrets.

That was the promise she'd made herself. And she would be an idiot and regret it until the end of her days if she didn't have him. Right now.

"Have your eyes finished eating me?" Zach's expression was wry.

Yes. She was staring again.

"Are there any more rules, Anna?"

The sly humour in his expression, the smile that quirked his mouth unnerved her. Anna was speaking before she realised, "Just one. We have until dawn. After that, it's over. We..." Had she just said that? Protection. She wanted protection from another of Zach's cynical offers. She watched his eyes narrow and her chest tightened. His humour had faded. "We...never mention it again. And after our week's up, we very happily go our separate ways." Her chin lifted. "Agreed?"

"Seems you're very used to brokering deals, Anna."

Zach could never resist the little stinging jabs. Even now. She glared up at him. Close. So close that his scent filled her, mixing with the fire in her blood. "You should be pleased that I'm not begging to be a chain around your neck."

"I'm not a fool, Anna." The low growl of his voice tore through her. His knuckles stroking her cheek jolted her. "The only place for you is in my bed." Fire sparked in his eyes. "And wherever else I can have you. Nothing more."

"I will never be one of your deals."

"No?" His smile was wicked. "Is that a dare?"

Her blood was in riot, heat burning her face. Anger or need... The lines were blurred. "You—"

"I'll take that as a yes." And his mouth crushed hers.

She should have remembered that talking was overrated. Completely overrated, when she could be doing this.

Her mouth opened and she sighed at the sweet taste of him, at the clever, clever flick of his tongue over hers. His hands slid down her body, shaping every curve until she was pressed against the hardness of his chest.

Anna groaned.

The satin heat of his skin against hers.

So simple.

But it shot fire through her veins. And then her hands started to move, to slide over his smooth skin, feel strong muscles tense under her fleeting touch. Her fingers pushed at the waistband of his trousers. Wanting, needing to feel more, all of him.

"Patience." His voice was a growl against her shoulder and she shivered. "We have until dawn, Anna." In one swift movement, she was high in his arms. A feral smile cut his mouth. "And if this is to be secret...? I want to make certain that it's a secret worth keeping."

Anna's mouth dried.

Zach laid her on his bed, sheets cool against her burning skin. She watched his fingers unbuckle his belt, tug at the button and zip on his trousers. She swallowed, suddenly nervous. Her heart pounded.

She'd had sex with this man, years ago. A brief, incredible moment.

But she had never seen him naked.

Anna's head fell back into the deep pillows and she made herself stare up at the ceiling. Follow the subtle moulding that edged it. Breathe. Breathe. Before she panicked. She wanted this. She did. But she was scared.

Her eyes closed.

Scared that she would make a fool of herself. That despite what she thought, a man like Zach would baulk at her inexperience.

"Anna?" The hot glide of his fingers across her stomach broke her thoughts. "Have I bored you already?"

He wanted her. She wanted him.

Anna shivered under the slow, sure caress. She made a smile curve her lips. "Not...yet."

Zach's reply was a hot, wet mouth on her stomach, his tongue tracing her navel. She yelped, wriggling. His laughter shot heat to her toes. "I think I know how to keep your interest."

That mouth, that tongue sliding lower, little kisses against her flesh.

In reflex, Anna grabbed at the pillows, arching her spine under his touch. Oh God... She had never done this.

"Just this tiny scrap of lace." His breath stirred her damp skin and his fingers pulled at the practically indecent underwear her sister had left her. Then all thought disintegrated. There was only his mouth and those insane little kisses.

The sudden heat of his tongue lifted her pelvis off the bed.

A strong hand held her down.

Fire pulsed low in her belly with each stroke of his tongue, the clever way he licked and sucked. Anna moaned against the perfect, perfect... Her blood pounded. Little bursts of pleasure fired through her brain. She couldn't take this. She couldn't. It was driving her insane, her body twisting, writhing.

But always strong fingers held her, finding her.

She was so close, so—

Dazed, she focused on the dark, tousled head buried between her thighs. Zach. To know it was Zach. Oh God. Oh—

A burst of heat rioted through her body, her blood singing, her mind lost to light. She thought she cried out his name.

But at that moment, she didn't care.

Nothing mattered.

Finally, finally her body sank into the soft mattress and a satisfied grin split her mouth.

"So that wasn't boring?"

"Interesting." Her voice was breathy and she couldn't help herself. "Very interesting. Would you like marks out of ten?"

"Flippant?"

The happy post-orgasmic buzz still held her. "Always."

"Not for long." His silver-edged gaze speared her. "I promise."

Her heart pounded, but she couldn't tear her attention away from him. Impossibly, a low throb pulsed again. She couldn't breathe. To see him slide over her skin, feel the heat, the weight of him on her body. It was just the first of her forbidden dreams...ones that started when she was nineteen. When Zach saw her as a woman, not Gregory's annoying problem.

No. She pushed all distractions from her mind. Focus on the now, on the here. Not those stupid thoughts whirling up from six years before.

"So what will you do to keep my interest this time?"

A wicked smile curved his mouth. "Where do I begin, Anna? So much to do. So little time. But I think I'll start here again."

The slow trail of his mouth tracing over her stomach. Open-mouthed kisses stealing over her ribs, flickering his tongue along the underside of her breast.

Anna hissed, caught unawares by the unexpected riot of sensation. Damn the man, his mouth should be outlawed.

"Like that, Anna?"

Warm breath prickled her skin, made her eyes crush against the very real need to grab him, roll him. The wantonness of her thoughts shocked her but she could feel him hard and long against her thigh. Everything in her yearned for him inside her.

"This isn't going to be quick. I made a promise."

Somewhere in her mind she heard his smile, but then that talented mouth had plans. "Zach..."

"So impatient, Anna."

"I—" The curl of his tongue around her nipple had her gasping.

"Now I *know* you liked that."

"Could you be more conceited?"

His low chuckle made her quiver. "I could always make you beg. In fact..." The run of his hot palm over her ribs, waist, curving around her hip sent fire through Anna's blood. "...I think I insist."

In that moment, everything screamed at her to do just that. Anna clung to her pride. "No games, Zach."

Darkness shadowed his gaze. "This isn't a game." The shift of his weight over her body, the warm brush of skin against skin was too much. Anna held back a groan. There was the snap of latex. "I want to know that you're...here...with me."

He'd pushed against her, her hips almost bucking in response. "What more proof do you need?" The words were gasped out on too little air.

"Say it."

He pushed harder and sensation screamed up her body. Not enough. Oh God, not nearly enough. Spots flickered against her eyelids, her spine arching, wanting, needing Zach to stop the torment. "*What?*"

"Say that you want this." His voice was rough, raw, his breath hot against her cheek. She was close, so very close. It had been so long. She was tight and the delicious pressure of him stretching her... "That you want...me."

Tremors took Anna's body, her fingers digging into his strong muscled arms. Heat swelled through her, her flesh throbbing—

"Say it, Anna."

—oh-God-oh-God-oh-God... "You. I want..."

Zach sank deep.

Her mind shattered. Her mouth took his, her arms crushing him, grinding against him in the fury of her overwhelmingly endless orgasm. She didn't care. She really didn't. It was complete insanity to want this man.

To love him.

The perfect clarity of that thought hit her. Swamped her with pain, with joy.

The crush of his body, his mouth buried in her neck and the blissful, blissful thrust of his hips. Yes. Love him. For six years. Possibly forever. Deeper. Already, more sweet heat tightened her flesh.

Deliberately, she shifted her body and he groaned, his fingers clutching at the bed sheets. Her hands found the hard muscle of his buttocks, urged him harder, faster.

"What are you doing to me, Anna?"

His dark, heated eyes held hers and she couldn't help the wicked smile that cut her mouth. "I'm going to make you beg."

"You..."

She took one of his nipples into her mouth and his words disintegrated. He shuddered under her touch. Muttered words, but Anna had little idea what he said. She was lost in the salty-sweet taste of his skin, the satin feel of it under grasping fingers. The way Zach groaned. And the incredible feeling of him deep, deep inside of her.

That single thought tore another sweep of heat through her flesh, made her cling to the man who cried out her name.

Gleaming eyes found hers, his trembling fingers stroking back her hair. "That was unfair," he murmured. He pulled a slow kiss from her lips. He rolled them, his arms squeezing tight around her body.

"I remembered," she said, her mouth brushing against his collarbone, breathing in the incredible scent of his hot, damp skin. She could feel the rapid thud of his heart slowing.

"We needed this, Anna." The press of his lips into her hair, the intimate gesture almost making her sigh. "To clear our heads. To realise this is nothing more than a stupid physical need."

The softly murmured words stabbed a hole where her heart used to be. Her body froze. She had to remember it had been her free choice. And with choice came the ability to make really idiotic mistakes. Her own bitter laugh echoed in her head. No. It hadn't been a moment of clarity. She couldn't love him. It was the rush of lust and heat. Nothing more.

"Anna?"

"A lust sated." The words were ash in her mouth. At least she hadn't been stupid enough to say those three little words, the ones that had burned on her tongue. "I should..."

"Where are you going?"

Where could she go? She wanted to run away, put miles between her and the warmth of his bed, his body and the scent of their love. Sex. It was only sex. She disentangled herself from his arms, swung her legs out of the bed. Her toes dug into the soft carpet. "I always sleep alone."

Zach stared at the smooth run of her spine and stopped himself from scrubbing at his face. It was good that she saw it the way he did. Wasn't it? He pulled off the condom and knotted it.

"Very sensible," he muttered, disappearing into the *en suite.*

She was still there when he got back. Damn.

He tugged at the sheet to cover himself. He had to get her out of the room. Because with each passing second his gaze strayed over the soft curve of her waist as it flared into her hip. And where it went, his mouth wanted to follow. He was an idiot. He had let his pride get in the way for too long. If he hadn't, she wouldn't have this power over him.

"So." He swallowed back in a dry throat. "The bedroom by the study."

She snorted. "You trust me now?"

"Are you going to run, Anna?" He couldn't stop the finger that traced the length of her spine. She quivered at his touch. "Honestly?" The agreement had been until dawn...but Anna had pulled back. Zach blinked. Had it all been an act?

His hand dropped away.

"If such a thing is possible," he murmured.

"Didn't think you did." Anna dropped to her knees on the floor and tugged on her dress, easing it down over her hips. She stood. The white silk almost gleamed in the low light of the room.

"Anna, I know you too well."

"Of course you do," she said. He lost her face to shadow. "And now it's in a bed too." She straightened. "It's the truth that I only want my house, Zach." She ran a hand through her hair. "And I never wanted this...mess. So I don't regret it. But in all *honesty*"—the word was twisted—"I wish it had never happened."

Her words were a punch to his chest. Was that a dent to his pride? Women fell over themselves for him. Now this woman, who had known so *many* men, was comparing him to them. A hot surge of anger swept through him. "Mess?"

Anna took a back step. Her thumb jabbed at the door behind her. "It's been a long day, so..."

Zach stared. "A long *day*?"

She swallowed and her attention fixed somewhere on the rumpled sheets. "Zach, this is already embarrassing enough."

"You were supposed to be in my bed until dawn, Anna."

A pale hand rubbed over her face. "I don't think that's wise, do you?"

Zach knew the sensible thing would be to let her go to that other room. He wanted her. Too much. But damn it, he should be the one backing away from a clinging female. He winced at that thought. Hardly something of which to be proud. "So you always run?"

Her dark gaze flickered over his but didn't stay. "I told you. There has only been you."

"Oh please, Anna." Zach threw away the sheet and his hand searched the floor for his underwear. "I didn't believe it this afternoon. I'm certainly not going to believe it now."

"Fine. Carry on thinking exactly what you like. I'm wasting the truth on you."

He stood and Anna bumped back into the closed door. "You started this." Her hand twisted hard at the handle and he couldn't help the smile that grew. "What? Nervous, Anna?" He planted his palms on either side of her, blocking her with his body. "This is all an act, isn't it? The naïve woman under the thumb of her sister." Her breathing was erratic as she stared up at him. That damned herbal scent fogged his brain.

"Six years ago." His voice was barely above a rough whisper. "I *might* have thought differently. But that was before I really knew you."

Her body radiated heat only inches from his own, firing over his cool skin. Just a little closer. Only a little...

"Zach?"

Why did he want her? Was it his lot that only the most unsuitable woman would drive him insane? Maybe it was genetic. He should go back to bed, forget everything about her...but then he lost himself in her dark brown gaze. "Stay."

What the...? Had he just said that?

"Stay?"

Yes. Seemed he had. Anna swallowed and her deepened breaths pushed against him. He almost hissed at the slide of her warm silk-covered breasts over his chest. "You want to." His hand curved against her jaw and he felt her lean into that touch. Sex. It was only ever about sex. And stupidly he didn't care whether hers was an act. "You know you do."

"I..." She had been leaving. She had. But now, with Zach pressing close, all sensible thought ended. "...should go—"

"—back to that bed?"

She didn't want to echo his smile. Her chest hurt and she had to say, "This doesn't mean anything."

His hand stilled on her cheek. "Does it have to? We're both single consenting adults."

For a full moment, Anna wished she were the woman he thought she was. Everything would be so much easier. And she wouldn't have the burning hole in her chest. "No."

"No?"

Zach's head dipped and his lips covered hers in a gentle caress that warmed down to her toes. His hands cupped her shoulders, their heat sinking into her cold skin. There was nothing else she wanted. Nothing.

Except his love.

Her heart contracted to a stone.

And she would never have that.

Anna tore her mouth away, twisted her head from him. "I can't do this."

Zach's tight breaths filled her senses. Why didn't he say something? Anything? His hands shot back. "Fine." She lost the warmth of his body. "More fool me for pushing the act."

"I wasn't acting." Anna's fingers covered her mouth. The urge to cry burned her eyes. "I...wanted to be with you. But..."

"It didn't live up to expectations?" Zach's voice was bitter.

"No, never—" Anna bit back more words. He would never know how she really felt. Never. She would not give him that power over her. "I have to go." She tugged at the door, feeling the handle give. "Good night, Zach."

She scrambled from the room. Get away. Get into that other bedroom, lock the door, collapse on the bed and try to ignore the *complete* fool she had made of herself.

Anna leant against the heavy door and stared into the softly lit room. She let out a weary breath. Her gaze skirted the wide bed. Sleep. She needed to sleep. And she prayed not to dream.

Sharp knocking jarred her spine.

"Anna. Open up. You didn't think you'd get away that easily... Did you?"

Chapter Nine

"So this is normally how you end your evenings?"

Anna stepped back. "What? Being chased by a half-naked man through his flat? Let me think. That would be a...no."

A hard smile dragged at Zach's mouth. "The act. The 'what have I done?' An easy way to escape without consequences."

"This is what you wanted, Zach." Anna folded her arms across her chest. "Walk-away sex."

A sour ache twisted his gut. Did she have to make it sound so...sordid? He wasn't going to admit to her how long it had been since he had sex. Nothing would drag that from him. Not when she'd probably had scores of men since *their* first encounter. And that brought out the old bitterness. "Your trademark I thought."

She was looking anywhere but at him. "Zach, can you leave so that I can go to bed?"

"How did you turn out like this?" He closed the bedroom door and leant against it. His hand rubbed over his bristled jaw. "I mean, you always seemed such a quiet, modest girl. And yet you became your sister."

A flush rose under her pale skin. His pulse jumped but he clamped his will onto it. His body already demanded more of her. He would be a fool to give into that impulse. No matter how tempting.

"I told you, Zach." She looked up and her dark eyes shone with the hint of tears. Just a hint. She had to be too tired to act further. "I keep telling you. I lied. I lied because I didn't want"—she jerked her finger between them—"this."

"This?"

The flush to her skin flared anger now. "You can't help yourself, can you?" She walked past him, heading for the *en suite*. "Get out, Zach. I'm going to scrub this muck off my face and get some sleep."

"No." His hand closed around her bare arm and a surge burned through him at the contact. Damn the woman. Why her? Why did he react so strongly to her? "Not yet."

"More insults?" Anna pulled her arm free. She glanced down and the redness in her face deepened. "But then *that* seems to be calling you a hypocrite."

"*That* is biological," Zach muttered. "Nothing more."

"Fine." The word had an edge to it. Her chin lifted. "Just find someone else to sort out your problem."

Zach stiffened. "My problem?"

What had she said now? His steel blue gaze pierced her and her heart thumped at the edge of ice it held. Heat burst through her. But, damn him, she was not going to be intimidated. Not anymore. "I'm not here to satisfy you."

A flush darkened his cheeks. "Believe me, you are the last woman I want." His look scorched a path down her body and it had her skin tingling. "The very last."

Her smile was sharp. "Is that why you're looking at me like that?" His attention shot back to her and hunger still lingered there. Anna wanted to ignore the responding tug. "Like you've forgotten what a woman felt like?"

"You're gloating?" The next words had a razor edge. "And you think it's funny."

"Why not?" Anna said. The burn in her blood made her reckless. "The high and mighty Zachary Quinn reduced to wanting...me."

He pushed himself away from the door. Anna stopped herself from taking a back step. "Is that why you rubbed my face in how many men you've had? And this latest lie. I'm now the 'last man you slept with'." His voice sneered. "Because you so enjoy twisting the knife." His laughter was short, bitter. "My God, Anna, you and Sofia really are from the same mould."

"I am nothing like her."

"Of course not." His large hand framed her jaw and heat bled into her cool skin. "You're just an innocent." His thumb teased her mouth, edging her lips with so light a touch it had her mind spinning. "Trapped by your scheming sister. Poor. Little. Anna." His hand snapped back. "Isabelle told you."

Her mouth burned from the press of this thumb and she still had the imprint of his touch on her jaw. Confusion clogged her thoughts. "Told me?"

"Obviously tonight had to have been a shock."

Zach and his usual understatement. "Yes."

He sank onto the edge of the bed. "Finally you're being honest."

What was he doing? "You were leaving," she murmured and she tried not to follow the smooth run of chest, his stomach muscles, to remember the heat of them over her own naked skin. She swallowed. "Zach?"

He looked up and what she found in him fired pain through her chest. Defeat. This wasn't Zach. He was indestructible. Panic bubbled through her and words burst out. "Gregory's will can be contested. A court will see it's crazy and we can get on with our separate lives. Zach? It'll be all right."

"Why reassure me about that, Anna? You've just secured a blank cheque for yourself, haven't you?" His soft laughter sounded strangely bitter. "Why should I be concerned about buying yet another woman's silence?"

Anna stared at him. "What are you talking about?"

"Stop this," he muttered. "This act."

"You're making no sense." She scrubbed weary hands over her face. "And for the very last time, I *do not* want your business, I *do not* want your money. I want..." Stupid words had almost tumbled out. Wanting him wasn't a part of the deal. "I want my house. That's it."

"Really?"

"Yes."

"And tonight, being here...sleeping...with me, wasn't what you planned?"

Anna paused. "Planned? No."

"You just couldn't help yourself."

"Don't..."

"Found the thought of seeing whether it was true too impossible to resist."

"What the *hell* are you talking about?"

"Me." Zach stood, towering over her, so close she could feel the heat of his skin and his scent wrap around her. "Disappointed that what you heard was false?"

"Have you gone insane?"

"Maybe."

Anna's spine hit the door.

"*Déjà vu*," he said.

"Zach?" She stared up into his darkening eyes and tried to pull coherent thoughts into her brain. But she could only feel the press of his long body against hers, the warmth through the thinness of her dress. One thought fixed in her head. Her stupid dress had to go. Her hips shifted involuntarily against his.

"See? I'm more than ready for you. Isabelle lied."

Hints dropped into place and now she understood.

His problem.

Isabelle was telling the world he was impotent.

Zach had always been a very private man, detesting publicity and holding a deep hatred of anyone knowing anything about him, or his private life. His lawyers had managed to gag Isabelle, stopping her from talking about their relationship in public...but in private?

"I can't believe it of Isabelle."

Zach laughed. "Why not?"

He traced her lip, her mouth burning at the light touch.

"Which one of *your* secrets would you like me to share?"

Her skin prickled. "She wouldn't... She didn't..."

"Isabelle laughed when she told me how you discovered—what was his name?—Iain something...was cheating on you. How you walked and walked, until you were drenched to the skin—"

Anna crushed her eyes shut. She had stupidly idolised Isabelle. "No."

"I'm sorry, Anna." The softness of his voice forced out an unexpected tear. He caught it, her eyelashes fluttering against his thumb tip. "She plays everyone."

"Just like you."

His hand stilled on her cheek. "Is that what you think of me?"

Anna snorted. "Haven't I told you often enough?" She let out a slow breath. "Zach…"

He had been offering comfort and she had slipped into her usual defense. Attack. The soft light shadowed his features and she was certain she wasn't imagining the wariness, the distrust in his face. Simple gossip, but gossip was Zach's greatest fear. Anna had known that for a long time. Had used it. Yes, Isabelle's vicious lies had scarred him.

The need to hold him, to promise that it would be all right, seared through her. Yet those words she couldn't speak. Zach wouldn't believe her. But she did have a way to show she cared.

Anna smiled. "We could be doing something much better than talking."

Her hands slid over his buttocks and urged him hard against her. The throb low in her flesh quickened and it was suddenly difficult to think.

"You're a piece of work…"

"Want me to stop?"

His low moan gave her her answer. She rubbed her pelvis over the hard length of his erection and heat licked. She swallowed. "Of course, you can leave, if you want." Her tongue tasted his skin. "But I'd much rather you stayed."

"Damn you, Anna." But his hands were already sliding down, down.

"No." She stopped them. Something flickered through his gaze and her heart squeezed. Pain. Hurt. "My way."

He blinked. "Your way? What's..." Anna pushed him back against the wall and air left his lungs at the impact. "...your way?"

Did the unflappable Zachary Quinn sound nervous? Anna smiled and traced a fingertip over his chin, slipping further and edging the sharp definition of his clavicle. Down. She ignored her nerves. He hissed as her nail circled his nipple. "A slow"—circling closer—"slow"—and closer until she flicked the nipple—"torture."

Zach groaned.

Her finger slid lower, tracing his muscled stomach, and she came to the edge of his boxer shorts. She pushed them lower over his hips until they dropped to his feet. "Now where was I?"

She placed an open-mouthed kiss on his shoulder, biting, licking her way to his nipple. Taking it into her mouth, she teased it between her teeth and grinned when Zach moaned. His fingers threaded through her hair.

Her tongue licked the curve of his pectoral and moved lower.

Zach formed a fist in her hair. "Anna. You don't have to..."

"My way, Zach."

His hand slipped away. She had to have imagined the tremor. "Do with me what you will."

Anna laughed against his stomach, felt his response in the ripple of muscle. The salt-sweet taste of his skin was addictive and her laughter faded. Touching him, letting her hands, her mouth slide and lose her fear in exploration. Anna wanted to do this for him.

She licked the underside of his erection.

Zach groaned, his body jerking.

Her hand closed around his penis and she took it into her mouth.

"Anna... Stop!"

Her gut twisted. What had she done wrong? God, she felt like such a naïve idiot. Strong hands pulled her up and she found herself wrapped tight against his chest.

"I thought...but it's been... And I don't..."

"Zach, you're making no sense."

His chest lifted as he let out a long sigh. "It's been...a while."

Anna froze. She swallowed. "You haven't...?" She pulled back to look up at him and found a dark embarrassed flush across his cheekbones. There was no emotion in his eyes. She didn't want to drag it out, but it was too hard to believe. "But Isabelle lied."

The flush deepened and a muscle jumped in his jaw. "Her lie spread. Gossip followed me. It was like old times... In the end it was easier to avoid getting involved." His mouth twisted and there was something bitter in his expression. "And cheaper."

"So you think that I want your money."

"Don't you?"

Anger put steel in her spine. The man made her crazy. "And what lie are you protecting? That you're *not* impotent?"

"I stopped having to play Isabelle's games when I divorced her." His gaze drilled her. "Or yours."

Her mouth thinned. There was something more. She could feel it.

"Why did you stop me?"

"Damn it, Anna, don't push. You were right, this is a mess."

"No. Tell me."

He grabbed his underwear. "Good night."

"No." Anna blocked the door. "*Tell* me."

Zach glared at her. "Move, Anna, or I *will* make you."

An insane pulse of excitement throbbed in her blood. The fire that had always burned between them flared again. His anger excited her. She knew now it always had. She pressed her body back against the solid door and met his glare. "Then make me."

"Anna." The threat in his voice only pushed her hands harder against the door. "Stop this."

Her smile was sharp. "Again. Make me."

He was close and she breathed in the scent of his skin, the scent of his arousal. "Is that what you want?"

She ran her fingers along the silken strength of his erection. His jaw clenched. "Dawn is still far off... But if you want to waste—"

"Stop talking." His mouth crushed hers, his tongue invading.

Everything else was forgotten.

Zach found the bed and stripped the silk dress from her body. He threw it to the floor. "How do you do this to me?"

He pushed at her heated flesh, tantalisingly close, so close that sweet tension flared. He just had to push a little harder...

"Do what?" Her hips tilted, wanting, needing more of him inside of her. Pushing, sliding, skin against skin. There. Oh God, there. Just... She grabbed at his buttocks, urging him deeper.

Zach buried his face against her neck, his breath sending shivers over her sensitive skin. "Anna, we really should—"

She rolled him.

Her mouth found his nipple and all argument stopped.

Faster. Zach's hands on her hips, holding her, urging her.

The tightening in her pelvis forced a moan. Almost. Oh God, almost... Little sparks of light fired through her brain and her body teetered on the edge—

Anna cried out.

The orgasm washed through her in a dizzying rush, endless, joyous.

Zach's mouth crushed hers and she swallowed his moans as he came.

The kiss eased into something slow, gentle. Anna pulled away with a sigh and rested her head on his shoulder. Her lips brushed his damp neck. He still smelt wonderful.

"Anna?"

"Hmm?" Already sleep tugged at her. Falling asleep wrapped in Zach's arms. Not the way she had seen the day ending. Her smile was wry. Not even the way she thought the past hour would end.

His breathing had slowed and whatever he wanted to say drifted away as his eyes closed. Anna snuggled into his chest and found the even thud of his heartbeat under her ear.

Its rhythm soothed her.

She would face the fallout for this in the morning.

Not before.

೫)೦೪

Anna sighed and stretched, a delicious heat building through her body. Was she imagining the delicate play of fingers over her stomach, her breasts? Oh, that was nice. Very, very nice.

She pushed her arms above her head and arched her spine.

A hot, wet mouth found the underside of her breast and she couldn't hold back the gasp. "Have I told you I love you today, Zachary Quinn?"

And she froze.

What the hell had she just said?

Had he heard? God, she was an idiot.

"Anna..." The loud ring of a telephone cut into his words. He cursed and threw back the covers. "I have to get that." He jabbed a thumb towards the door. "But we are going to talk." He grabbed his underwear and left.

Anna collapsed back into the warmth of the bed, the light stinging her eyes. Zach's scent clung to the pillow, the sheets, her skin. She groaned and scrubbed at her face. "I'm an idiot." What had possessed her to admit that she loved him?

And she did. Probably always had.

She stopped herself from groaning again.

Now he was going to come back from his phone call and want to discuss it.

"Over my dead body."

Anna leapt from the bed. She glanced at the clock. Just after three.

No, she couldn't just run... The shower. She would make it look like she was in the shower. She ran into the *en suite* and snapped on the showerheads. Cool water spurted over her arm, face and she shivered. Her reflection caught her and for a moment she stopped and stared at the stranger she'd become.

Tangled hair, swollen lips and a knowing in her eyes that had never been there before.

Anna shook her head and pulled the frosted cubicle doors shut.

No time to delay. She had to escape.

And damn it, her clothes were everywhere.

She threw on the dress. Her feet were silent in the thick carpet but her gut still curled tight with fear. She had to get away. The over-loud click of the twisting doorknob made her hiss...and then she was outside the room in the relative safety of the hall.

Her tight breathing eased.

Find her bag, find her shoes and run.

But she had to pass the study. Its door was shut and she could hear Zach's heated voice. Someone else was having their ear chewed off. Anna scratched a trembling hand through her tangled hair and quickly retraced the path to his bedroom.

The scent of *them* still pervaded that room too.

Not looking at the crumpled sheets, Anna snatched up her sandals. Her face burned as she picked up her discarded underwear and headed for the drawing room. Her bag. Get her bag and escape. She held back a curse. Her bag was in the study.

Everything had gone to hell...but if she could just get home and explain to Sofia. Maybe her sister would see sense.

The front door clicked softly shut behind her.

Anna sprinted for the lift.

When the doors had closed with a gentle whoosh, she collapsed back against the cold rail. Sofia had to see sense. And she would.

She slid her feet into the uncomfortable sandals. She had no cash for a taxi. Her mobile. Anna remembered exactly where her phone was and her face flushed.

She ran her fingers through her tangled hair and her mind raced.

Standing out in the road in the hope of a black cab passing by at such an ungodly hour wasn't an option. Wandering the streets for a phone box was equally unappealing. She let out a slow sigh. The doorman would be able to call a taxi for her. She could scrounge money when she got back to Ashford.

The lift doors pinged and Anna stopped herself from cursing.

Luck never ran with her.

"Can I help you?"

Her gut tightened at his note of professional concern. She had to look a mess. But she stitched on her social smile and met the man's light gaze. "Can I use your phone, please?"

He blinked. "Of course, miss."

Her fingers hovered over the buttons. Not a taxi. Freddie. He was the safest option. Freddie would get her home. He would let her slump, let her stare out of the window and not offer constant and annoying chat.

"Freddie?" She winced at the sleepy tones at the other end of the line. "I need a lift."

"Are you okay?" His tiredness fell away and worry replaced it.

"Fine. Just..." She turned away from the sharp gaze of the concierge and watched the closed doors of the lift. "...hurry."

ℰᏣ

Tyres screeched away and Anna's head fell back against the headrest.

She was doing the right thing. She was.

Sofia had no interest in Zach's company. She would help to overturn Gregory's crazy will. Anna held tight to that belief. It was the only way she was getting away from Zach.

The other time she had run from him burned through her memory.

Soft, slow kisses brushed her skin as the rush of her orgasm ebbed away. She had been right to come to him; right to push for more when he had withdrawn from her...

"Zach?"

"Hmmm?"

The slide of his mouth over her skin coursed little shivers. "What happens now?"

"What do you mean?"

Those absent words had her heart tightening. Had she just been an easy screw up against his drawing room wall? Anna crushed her eyes against that thought. "Is that it?"

His mouth stopped. Hands slid from her body and she dropped to the floor on clumsy feet. Zach's expression was wary as he tucked his shirt back into his trousers. "What else were you expecting, Anna?"

Oh God, she had been a complete and utter idiot. To save herself she said, "Nothing. Obviously."

"Then we must reach a financial agreement."

"You want to buy me?" Anna straightened her dress with quick hands. She glared at Zach and strode to the door. She tossed words at him. *"You could never afford me!"*

And she ran.

"What happened?"

Freddie's voice pulled her out of unwanted thoughts.

"Not now, Freddie, please," she murmured. The glass reflected her pale face and her eyes lost to the darkness. "I'm tired." That wasn't a lie. A flare of pink burned over her cheeks. Her body ached in places she never suspected she *could* ache. "Just tired."

"What did he do?"

A weary laugh escaped her. "Big brother strikes again."

"Did he hurt you?"

That was a loaded question. "No, Freddie. I'm fine." She turned her head. "I am. It's just that he's not going to be...very happy with me."

"He never seemed very happy with you." Her friend's voice was just above a rough whisper and his knuckles whitened around the steering wheel. "Obsessed. But not happy."

Freddie's words chilled her. "Obsessed?"

"He always looks at you the same way...as if he could eat you alive." The car pulled sharp away from the lights, tearing across the empty junction. "But then you look at him that way too."

"I do not."

Freddie gave a soft chuckle. "Anna, how long have I known you?"

"Forever?"

"Forever," he agreed. "You look at him that way too."

"I'm not talking about this." She turned her head back to the dark, empty streets. Of course she knew that she craved Zach. Wanting him was as necessary as breathing. And now that she'd tasted more of him... No. She definitely didn't want to talk about it.

Familiar landmarks jumped out at her. All too soon, she would be able to curl up in her own bed and just sleep. She felt weary down to the bone.

The car slowed and Freddie turned it into the drive, the tyres thankfully silent over the even cobbles. Her house keys? No bag...so there was a side door key under the sprawling hebe bush. That problem solved, her mind slid thankfully to thoughts of the quiet sanctuary of her bed.

Until she saw him.

Adrenalin surged and blood flared in her face.

She was an idiot.

Of course her home would be the first place he would look for her. But all her thoughts had been on running. "I'm a complete idiot," she muttered under her breath.

"Anna?"

She shook her head. "Go home, Freddie. I shouldn't have gotten you involved in this mess." She gave him a forced smile. "Not again." She willed her hand to open the passenger door. The chill, early morning air made her shiver. "Go. I'm fine."

"No."

"I have to sort this."

"Call me," Freddie said, his face harsh. "As soon as he's gone. Call me."

Anna stepped away from the small car and watched him reverse out of the drive. Then she had to turn her attention back to the man waiting for her.

He lounged against his car door like some big cat. Relaxed but dangerously alert. Her heart thumped. Hard. She willed her legs to move forward and her heels clicked over stone.

Zach didn't move.

His arms stayed folded across his chest and his gaze remained fixed on her. The light over the door cast a bright, white shine over his features, throwing his face into harsh relief. He didn't look angry. Anna suspected he had passed anger and then probably fury when he found her trick with the shower. His stony expression screamed cold hatred at her.

He pulled her mobile phone out of his trouser pocket. "Want to phone Petersen?"

Excuses burned on the tip of her tongue. She decided against them. "I wasn't thinking."

"You were so overwhelmed you just had to get away?" His voice dripped with sarcasm. "Yes. I often have to chase women halfway across town after I've had sex with them."

Anna's face flushed. "Can we go inside?"

Zach uncoiled his body from his sleek car and Anna had to stop herself from flinching. She fixed her feet to the ground. He was close, so close that the warmth of his breath brushed her. "I also had to answer your phone and find that another man was waiting for you."

"Freddie called my phone."

"Yes. Freddie called your phone." His fingertip followed a path along her jaw. "*Déjà vu,* Anna."

Her skin prickled at his touch, sending a new shiver through her cold skin.

"You're cold." He shrugged out of his leather jacket and draped it over her shoulders. Instant warmth flooded her. His unique scent mixed with soft leather had her senses reeling, as did his unexpected gesture of concern. She knew she was really tired then, because tears burned.

"Thank you," she murmured, slipping her arms into the still warm leather and pushing down the tight pain of imagining that Zach would hold her so close. "We...we should go inside."

"No."

"I'm not going back to your apartment, Zach."

His jaw shifted, in the cold silence she was sure she could hear his teeth grind together. His voice was unnaturally soft. "So you're breaking the agreement."

"Sofia will see reason. If I ask her. This will end right here."

Zach's bark of hard laughter cut through the night air. "Sofia can't wait to get her hands on my company. You both can't."

"That is not true."

"Please, stop the games, Anna. You're doing all of this for a miserly plot of land and a half-derelict house? I don't think so."

"My mother restored—"

"I know the history." Zach sliced into her words. "And no one would go as far as you have for that."

Pain burned. "Go as far as I have?" she repeated, almost choking on the words.

A tight smile slashed his mouth. "Did you panic at that part of the plan?" His gaze slid down her body, delayed on her abdomen. "There's no way I'd pay you off. Or allow an abortion."

Panic shot to her toes. In her race to get away, she hadn't given it a thought. They hadn't used a condom and she didn't take any form of contraception. There was no need. Frantic dates ran through her mind. She was safe. She was sure.

What he implied hit her dazed brain. "I would never do that."

"Of course." His smug expression had her hand itching to fly at him. "And we're back to you being overwhelmed. But..." his gaze fixed on her abdomen again, "...if there is a baby—"

"There isn't."

"So you're protected?"

The promise to herself of no longer lying chaffed. She closed her eyes. "No. But I didn't plan this."

He gripped her arm. "If you're pregnant you'll find yourself stuck with me a lot longer than a week."

For a moment, a stupid rush of joy coursed through her, but the spike of disgust in his tone killed it. She tugged her arm free. "I'm not going back."

"Even if I have to throw you over my shoulder and carry you back on foot, we will meet the conditions of this insane will." His voice was no more than a growl. "Now get in the car."

"No."

"Anna..."

"Can you two not stay away?"

Anna groaned. Not her. Not now. "Sofia."

"Anna thought she'd forgotten something. Turns out she hadn't," Zach said. He waved the car keys at her. "Bye."

Sofia smirked. She pulled the belt of her silk dressing gown tighter around her waist. "What was so important at"—she glanced at her watch—"three-thirty in the morning? You always have a pack of twelve tucked in your bag."

"That's a lie, Sofia, and you know it," Anna muttered.

"Have you had to increase?" Her smirk widened. "But then you *are* popular."

"You're disgusting."

"You're the one who jumps any man who asks."

"Enough, Sofia," Zach grated. His hand took hers and Anna fought the need to squeeze it tight, to find comfort and strength in his touch. In that instant, she was more than happy to get into the car. "We're leaving."

"And another crashes before your charms." Her laughter was brittle. "Men are so easy to dupe, aren't they, Anna? They so rarely think with their brains. You can now add the great Zachary Quinn to your long list."

"Don't you get tired of lying?" Anna asked.

"Am I lying?" She straightened and smoothed over the rumpled silk of her dressing gown. "This was planned from the very beginning." Her smile was arch. "And when you grow bored..." her gaze raked over Zach, "...we must swap again."

Zach stopped. "What?"

"Didn't you know about my sister and Gregory?"

And with that, Sofia slammed the front door.

Chapter Ten

Anna snatched the keys from Zach's lax grip and scrambled into the car. The key found the ignition and she gunned the engine.

Zach slammed the passenger door. "What the hell do you think you're doing?"

"Getting out of here."

He only had time to grab at the seat belt before she roared the car out of the drive. Her face was pale, tight, and the grip she had on the steering wheel screamed that she wanted to throttle someone. Sofia first. Then him.

He expelled a slow breath but there was still that fist in his gut. "So you and Gregory...?"

He was certain she was cursing, muttered words he couldn't catch. "I'll never forgive her for that."

The fist crushed. Nausea rose. "Then it's true?"

Her gaze shot to him, filled with acid. "You could believe that of me? God, I knew you thought I'd sleep with anything in trousers... But Gregory, too?"

"Why should he be exempt?"

"Because he's the only father I've ever known!"

Zach winced. His anger had lashed those words at her and she hadn't deserved them. "Anna, I'm sorry."

A bitter laugh, sharp, short burst from her. "Too late, Zach. You believed it. And you probably needed to."

Needed to have the image of her and Gregory fixed in his mind? He shuddered. "That's the last thing I want."

He already had the years' old image of her and Freddie seared into his brain. Discovering them on a broad couch in the garden room at Gregory's house, the boy already undressing her.

The murmur of Freddie's voice as Anna giggled...it had burst a fierce rage through him. Another betrayal. Another one.

"Anna."

The laughter, the murmurs stopped.

She swung a long leg down, shifting over the boy's lap in a way that made Zach grit his teeth. She stood. Her eyebrow lifted. "Hello, Zachary."

Something within him withered at the use of that name. It was the name Isabelle used. The one he had come to loathe. Now Anna followed her. "Don't ever call me that."

She shrugged. "No need to be so touchy. Zachary."

Anna smiled and Zach could have sworn she was taking lessons from his ex-wife. It chilled him. He had misjudged Anna. She wasn't the woman he thought she was. Pain hitched in his chest, forcing a sour anger through his blood. "Get dressed."

"Why?" She stared down at her bare shoulder, her half-exposed breast. "It's nothing you haven't seen before."

The boy was grinning.

Zach took a controlling breath. He would not lose his temper. Not over her. "And you, out. Now."

"This isn't your house, Zach. And Gregory told me I can invite anyone I want. And I want Freddie."

Rage boiled through him. His hands balled into fists and still the boy grinned at him. Couldn't the idiot see that this woman was poison? Zach was only thankful that he had found out now. That he hadn't made a fool of himself. Again.

"Another itch you have to scratch?"

Anna turned away. "Freddie, I won't be a minute."

The boy's grin dimmed and something cold and hard entered his expression. He stood, moving close, and his hand briefly touched Anna's jaw. "Are you sure?"

Her fingertips brushed over the back of Freddie's hand. The intimate gesture hollowed Zach's chest and he had to look away.

"I'll be fine." She waited until he left before she turned back to him. Fire burned through her gaze. "Get out, Zach."

"No." He closed the distance between them. Anna continued to glare at him, her spine straight. "What the hell are you doing, Anna?"

"You don't own me."

His finger skimmed the edge of her jaw, tracing over Freddie's touch. The muscles tightened. Had she just flinched? Zach's fingers dropped away and his arm fell to his side. "Cover yourself up."

"You have no say over what I do."

"Is this who you want to be? Just like—" He stopped before he compared her to his ex-wife. "All right, Anna." This was yet another business deal with a woman. Nothing more. Zach made himself believe it. "We can make a deal. We continue, with the agreement from you it's on an exclusive basis. I will fund—" The flicker of horror across her face dried his words, dried his mouth. So that was a no. He pulled out his wallet and extracted one of his business cards. He held it out to Anna who just stared at it.

"*Contact my office. As I said before, we can come to a financial arrangement. On the understanding that you are never to speak of what happened between us. Agreed?*"

Anna's face flushed. She walked towards the open doors leading out to the broad lawn. Slow fingers shifted over her loose top, covering her shoulders. "*Your privacy must be protected at all costs.*"

He didn't miss the edge of sarcasm to her voice. "*Yes. You know that.*"

And then she muttered the words that had punched a hole through him. Turning, her face set hard, she said, "*No. You know what? I'd rather give it away for free, to* anyone *who asks, than be* paid *for anything by you.*"

Zach had no memory of how he had gotten out of Gregory's house after that.

His hand scrubbed at his face.

It had made him crazy. The guilt of how he had acted towards Freddie Lewis, despite his offer earlier that night, still gnawed at him. And now she was playing more games with him.

A sign for the M25 flashed past. "Where are you going?"

"Home."

"Home?"

"Let me show you why I'm doing this."

"Do I have a choice?"

Anna's grin was sharp before she turned her attention back to the road. "No. Doesn't look like," she said.

॰ॱ

She was insane. What was she doing spending more time alone with Zach? But here she was, splashing a once immaculate and powerful sports car down a twisting, mud-thick lane. It'd been years since she had last bolted to this house.

Six to be exact.

She held down a yawn and her eyes burned. Being so tired made the whole situation faintly ridiculous. "Not far now."

"Is all of this mud mine?"

He was the most annoying man on the planet. "Yes," she said.

"Nice."

Anna ignored him. She adjusted her grip on the steering wheel and focused hard on the slippery road. It was starting to look familiar and that fact burned in her chest. She couldn't lose this land to Sofia. Her sister wanted to tear down their old home and build a holiday park. Had for years. And that wasn't going to happen.

Anna pulled the car into a shallow cutting in the road and switched off the engine. Her arms, neck, spine ached. She'd been driving for hours and she wanted to sleep. Sleep for a week. She laughed to herself. At least that would get her out of her current problem.

"Care to share?" Zach asked.

"No," she murmured. She rubbed a cold hand over her stiff neck. "The entrance is just up the way but this car won't take us any further."

Anna climbed out of the low car and stretched her stiff back. The air was fresh and cold and she pulled Zach's heavy coat around her body. His scent invaded her and she breathed past it. An icy breeze rasped over her bare legs. Anna looked down. Her stupid shoes were already sinking into the mud and soft grass.

"This way."

Anna tottered to the old gate. She had the vague memory of tumbling off it head first in the mud when she was a child and her mother picking her up, holding her so tight and promising that everything would be all right...

"Anna?"

She could even smell her mother's light floral perfume.

"Anna?"

She willed away the pressure in her throat, her jaw. It shouldn't hurt this much. But it did. "Yes." She forced the word out and made herself push at the gate. "The house is behind that line of trees."

The grass brushed cold and wet over her bare toes, her heels sinking into the soft earth. What was she doing here? The anger of a few hours before had faded. Now she was in a sodden field, heading for a house with no heating, running water or food. Her stomach grumbled at that thought.

She should head back to the car, drive to the motorway services she'd sped past at dawn. Yet, she couldn't. She wanted Zach to see her home, needed him to understand. This was a place where she had been happy. She would never sacrifice that.

"How long has it been empty?"

Zach's voice made her start. She tugged his coat more securely around her body. "Over fifteen years now. My mother...my parents died and Sofia couldn't see herself living in the wilderness." Anna shrugged. "She was nineteen. It was sold."

"Wasn't it held in trust?"

"There were debts, Zach. The house and land were mortgaged to the hilt." She stepped over a thick clump of grass, her attention fixed on it, helping to hold back the pain, soured with time. "My father married for money. Then proceeded to spend it." Her laugh was bitter. "Now you see where Sofia gets her ideas."

"And you."

"No." She scratched at her tangled hair. "I'm nothing like her."

Anna pushed on ahead. This was a mess. She shouldn't have come here. Not her home. Not with him. At least he hadn't mentioned those three stupid words she'd uttered. The embarrassed heat held back the cold.

She pushed through the thick bushes and spikes of low branches and stopped. Anna stared. For a moment, an insane moment, she was nine again.

This was impossible.

At the bottom of the gentle slope and beyond the little apple orchard, sat her house. *Her* house. The one she remembered from her childhood. A higgledy-piggledy entrance, with the wide front door set back and lost to shadow. The old barn annex stretched off to the right. The numerous high chimneys...six years ago most had fallen through the ruined roof.

Six years before, she had stumbled through weeds and found the front door hanging by one hinge. Now, shaped shrubs edged the lawn and spring flowers burst up from tidy borders.

Slow feet took her forward.

Someone had restored it. Anna wiped at wet eyes and choked back more tears. Gregory had done this.

She stood before the front door, painted the exact pillar-box red she remembered. Her arm stretched up as she never could as a child and felt along the wood ledge above the door...until she found the hole. Inside was a key.

"Anna?"

Her hand shook.

Zach took the key from her and opened the front door. "Inside."

She was already moving. It was the same...and not. Anna had the more recent memory of debris and decay and only the hazy recollection of her childhood. Gregory hadn't replicated the interior precisely. But it was beautiful.

Her heels clicked over the stone flooring of the entrance hall, leaving clumps of damp soil and grass. She flopped onto a sofa set before the inglenook fireplace. "This is incredible."

"Yes."

Anna's head snapped up. "Did you know about this?"

"No." Zach stared around the low-beamed ceiling, the whitewashed walls. "But it's the sort of thing Gregory would do."

Anna scrubbed at her face for a final time, ridding it of any more tears and stood. "Yes. It is. So..." her hand waved around the little room, "...this is why I agreed to Gregory's insane will." Anna could feel the heat in her cheeks. This really was stupid. To drag them both out here. Zach didn't care. The heat flared in her cheeks. He'd had what he wanted.

"Anna..."

That tone. The "we need to talk" tone she had to avoid. "I wonder what else he's done." She fled through one of the doors leading into the rest of the house.

Every room was an immaculate blur until she ended up in the kitchen. Early morning light splashed through the long bank of windows opening out onto the kitchen garden. Anna leant against the cool granite of the central island and took slow breaths.

She had made everything worse.

Everything.

Her stomach growled. Yes, she could make a complete hash of her life, but her body still needed to be fed.

The large fridge was humming, so there was the possibility of food.

Cool air washed over her body and she stared at the well-stocked shelves. "You think of everything, Gregory," she murmured. "Except this mess."

Anna lifted a two-pint bottle of milk from the fridge door and looked at the date. Another week.

"You said you loved me."

The date blurred and she willed her hand to grip the plastic handle. "Yes."

Not lying anymore. Whose stupid idea had that been?

Anna put the milk on the island and turned to the cupboards. Tea. Falling into the familiar routine of making a pot of tea would settle her. She found a row of white mugs and a tea caddy in a cupboard beside the Belfast sink.

Had that shut him up?

Good.

She was aware of him on the edge of her vision, standing at the window, staring out into the garden.

"Yes?"

She splashed water into the kettle and switched it on. "You were there."

"Damn it, Anna. Is it something you always say?"

"Can we not analyse this?"

"Fine."

The kettle steamed and switched off. Anna poured it over a white pot. "We grab breakfast and then we head back. I'm sure you have something to do in your office."

"Yes." Zach pulled her mobile phone from his pocket and tapped in a number. "But first I'm sorting this stupidity out." He strode from the kitchen.

Anna stared after him, but then forced her attention back to the pot. No regrets. No recriminations. Soon she would have her house and Zach would be a fading memory. "Should have stopped thinking about him years ago. Got on with my life." She poured milk and then tea into a mug. Weariness weighed on her body and she didn't want to think of how it ached in unaccustomed places as she leant back against the granite worktop. The mug warmed her cold hands. "Maybe that's easier said than done."

Cereal and a good scrub, that was her plan. She would leave Zach to think he was being proactive.

Anna was halfway through her cornflakes when Zach reappeared.

"Carl Petersen's heading into his office. We have to meet him."

Her spoon stopped and she forced herself to swallow. "Meet him?"

"Sofia told him."

"What?"

He scraped a chair over the tiled floor and sat opposite to her. "What, she told him? Or what, what did she tell him?"

"Funny, Zach." Anna stirred her spoon through the debris of her breakfast. She was too tired for this. "What *could* Sofia have told him?"

"She saw you arrive with Freddie."

Could the morning get any worse? "So he wants to tell us the bad news in person."

Zach ran a hand through his untidy hair. "There is no way either of us is driving anywhere. David's picking us up."

"Gregory will have a penalty system. He wouldn't be able to stop himself from another little dig. You know that, don't you?"

He sat back and released a slow breath. "Very likely."

"You're taking this well."

"I am, aren't I?"

Anna gritted her teeth. "Zach. Stop it." The spoon clanked into the bowl. "I'm getting a shower..." The sudden shine to his eyes dried her words. She swallowed and hated that reaction.

"You denied me a shower."

The soft promise in his voice prickled her skin. "This is over, Zach."

"Is it?"

She stood. She was tired and grubby. And he was being a royal pain. "Yes. It is. We both know it. I was stupid to let it go that far."

"So..." Zach pushed himself out of his chair, "...if I were to suggest that I stink and I couldn't possibly manage to scrub *everywhere* clean...?" His grin was sharp.

Anna took a back step and refused to acknowledge the heat spreading under her skin. "You're perfectly capable of washing yourself. You're a grown man."

"Yes. I am."

He edged around the table that still separated them. Anna heard clicking and realised it was her shoes as she continued to retreat from him.

"You want to hide yourself away. Shouldn't you start to lay down some new memories here?"

"Not with you."

His face darkened. "Not with me?"

Anna smacked into a wall and the air whooshed out of her lungs. She winced. "Zach." The doorjamb was hard under her fingers. She shuffled sideways and found the open door. "We can go our separate ways."

His eyebrow lifted. "Is that what you want?"

He couldn't ask her questions like that. "Come on, be sensible. I've never been the woman you wanted."

"I beg to differ."

Anna's heart squeezed. "Don't play these games."

"Games?" He reached out to stroke her jaw. It stopped her dead. "Why would I play games, Anna? What would be my reason?"

Something itched. The tone of his voice wasn't quite...right. "What did Carl say? Exactly?"

"Gregory *did* have a penalty for not even lasting twenty-four hours." Zach's smile was sharp. "Of course, this is on top of losing everything." He stared at his hand, followed his finger as it traced her skin. "Petersen revealed one of Gregory's secrets."

Anna's stomach knotted. "Secrets?"

"One of your secrets, I should say."

"My...?" A shiver ran over her skin and she took a step back from him. Gregory couldn't know anything about her and Zach. He couldn't. "What did he say?"

"Did you think it was funny?"

Light angled across his face, throwing it into harsh relief. Suddenly, he was too close, too cramped in the narrow corridor. "Zach, I don't know what he told you..."

"I'm sure you do."

Anna stopped herself from running a hand over her unbrushed hair. "Do you want to drag this out any further? Or are you going to tell me?"

Zach's expression was carved from granite. "Freddie Lewis. You and him. It was a joke."

Anna blinked. She had never told Gregory anything. The false engagement had been a ploy to drive Zach away from her. In the panicked days after she'd first had sex with Zach, it was the only way she could see to escape him. She'd been an idiot. She'd known that for too many years.

She straightened. "It wasn't a joke."

"You meant me to find you half-dressed with him?" Anger beat hard in his voice and his skin flushed.

Thank you, Gregory... Anna made herself say the word. "Yes."

Zach blinked. "Why?"

The question surprised her. No sarcasm. Nothing witty. Just a simple question, so hard to answer. "You wanted to pay me. I am not a prostitute." Anna sighed. "Look, contest the will—"

He was staring. "You slept with him, with all of them, to spite me?"

"Zach, can we not have this conversation?"

His hand covered his mouth and for a moment, his shoulders slumped. He let out a slow breath. Anger curled around the next word. "Anna—"

His pocket started to ring. He cursed and answered it. "It's for you."

Anna took the mobile, trying not to touch Zach. "Hello?"

"Ms. Shrewsbury." Carl Peterson's voice crackled. "Mr. Quinn has no doubt informed you of the further penalty of not meeting the terms of Gregory Brabant's will. I…" He paused and there was an uncomfortable silence. Anna stared at her feet and controlled her breathing. "I am instructed to tell you that Mr. Quinn destroyed your friend's career six years ago."

"What?" The word was strangled. She stared at Zach. "Freddie?"

Without thought, her hand lashed his cheek and Zach staggered back from the blow.

Anna stabbed at the phone. Waved it at him. "You ruined Freddie."

"Yes."

One word. Cold. Callous.

Anger flared. She had never known. All those years and Freddie had never told her. "You don't care that you destroyed him? That it's taken years for him to resurrect his life, his career. *Years.* I had to use Sofia's whim to give him his major show." Tears edged her eyes. "You blackened his name."

"Yes." Zach's mouth flattened. "I had hoped it would teach him not to associate with women like you. Seems neither of us could learn that lesson."

Anna turned away from him before the urge to smack him again overcame her.

"Yes, do what you do best, Anna. Run."

She stopped. Her shoulders lifted. "Would you rather I hit you again?"

There was the rub of his hand over his bristled jaw. Zach's voice was sardonic. "You've had practise."

He had destroyed Freddie's life. The thought spun through her mind. This was Zachary Quinn. Proud. Self-righteous. But never underhanded. "I really don't know you, Zach, do I?" Her fingers caught in her hair and she made herself turn to face him. "He's still blacklisted. His friends fell away—"

"You didn't."

"No. I thought I'd gotten him into trouble. I never, for one minute, suspected you would do such a thing."

"I don't forgive."

Punching him, that felt really good right then. Her hand balled into a fist. Anger heated her words. "Me. Fine. But not him. He was—" Anna broke off.

"What, Anna?"

She couldn't say Freddie had offered her protection from Zach. Let him think it was spite. Better than the other reason. The one even Freddie didn't know about, that she was trying to protect her heart from Zach.

And failing.

"It was my idea." What truth she could tell him tasted raw in her mouth. "I was stupid. But I was the one you should have blamed, not him."

"I wanted nothing more to do with you."

"Yes." Her smile was sharp. "That's been evident."

"Funny."

Anna turned from him. She was too tired to stay and fight with him. She wanted a shower, to scrub herself clean and try not to think what other little surprises could be waiting for her in Gregory's will. "Contest the will, Zach. Get your business back. Just leave me out of it."

Zach grabbed her arm. "Suddenly, you don't care?"

Anna shrugged herself free. "All that I want now is a shower and sleep."

"Sleep then." He paused. "But we will talk, Anna."

"Yes, about how you're going to make it up to Freddie." Anna threw the words back at him and her heels clicked along the narrow corridor to the back stairs. "Let's talk about that, shall we?"

"And why you needed to use him."

Her hand closed around the newel post and it stopped the tremor.

"Is that a yes?"

Anna couldn't answer.

Chapter Eleven

"Anna."

She pushed her hair from her face and stretched, still only half awake. But the voice seemed insistent. Odd, it wasn't Sophia with her usual list of gripes. She curled back into the too-comfortable mattress. Not Sophia. So she could ignore it.

"Anna."

Warm fingers brushed over her cheek in a slow caress.

Anna sighed and leant into the touch. She wanted to imagine one man's hand there—

Her eyes shot open. "Zach." She yanked the crumpled duvet over her nakedness, gripping it beneath her chin. Her face burned scarlet. "Get out."

"Carl Petersen just phoned."

The colour faded from her face and she picked at the ironed cover of the duvet. "What's he said now?"

Zach couldn't help the hard smile. He stood. And tried not to remember the silky curve of her very bare flesh. "More dark secrets you're hiding?"

"Probably nowhere as many as you."

"Possibly." He stared out of the wide window, following the line of oaks bordering a mud-thick lane. It was easier. He couldn't look at her. "He just wanted to confirm that we hadn't killed each other."

"There's still time."

He ran his fingers through his damp hair. He'd showered and shaved. It still unnerved him that Gregory had stocked the bathroom cabinet with his brand of razors. That wasn't the only thing he'd found.

Had it been his old friend's plan to try to push them together? However, he and Anna had too much history, too many sour memories. Nothing would make them work. He should accept it.

Anna broke into his thoughts.

"David also rang. He's somewhere south of Canterbury. So he's about twenty minutes away."

Anna shrugged into a white dressing gown and wrapped the belt tight around her waist.

Accept it and walk away.

But morning sunlight edged her soft features and sleep had tousled her hair. Zach wanted to stroke the blush to her cheek, trace her mouth... Yes, walking away wasn't that easy. It never had been. He scrubbed at his face. He needed sleep. He wasn't thinking straight.

"He didn't reveal more of our dirty little secrets, if that's what you're worried about."

Anna masked a yawn. "I need coffee."

She padded out of the bedroom without a backward glance.

Zach ignored the tight fist in his chest. Damn the woman. If he *was* to walk away, he needed answers. He knew now he'd wanted them for six long years. "Anna."

"Coffee." She waved her hand and increased her pace down the stairs.

His solicitors were already working to overturn Gregory's ridiculous will.

He had only twenty minutes before his chauffeur turned up.

She *would* tell him the truth.

Anna made herself look busy. The last thing she wanted to do was talk to Zach. He was hovering in the doorway. Emotion bubbled and she focused on the kettle, willing it to boil. She would remain calm.

"Why did you use him?"

"Can we leave this?" She tore open a packet of coffee and dumped scoops into the French press. She was in control. He would not get to her. "I'm reconciled to losing the house." Her smile twisted. "Stupid to hang onto the past. Even if Gregory tried his best to make this place a home again."

"Why did you use him?"

Again, he asked the question in calm, measured tones.

With too much force, Anna squashed the coffee. She took an easing breath and poured it into a mug. She drank it black and shuddered. "Asking me the same thing over and over—"

"Why him?" He took the mug from her hand and put it back on the counter. "I deserve to know."

The arrogant— Anna bit down on the fury that wanted to explode against him. "I owe you nothing."

"What did you want to prove?" He lifted an eyebrow and there was a harsh glitter to his gaze. "That *anyone* was preferable to me?"

Anna stared at the mug, itching to pick it up again. She needed to do something with her hands. "No."

Zach's fingers on her jaw made her look at him. "Why?"

"Because you used me!"

Anna wrenched herself free. Stupid to say that. Stupid.

"Used you?"

She tried to retreat but Zach stalked her down the long kitchen. Today, there was nowhere for her to run. He would not get the truth out of her. She would not give him the satisfaction of knowing her feelings. How he would laugh then. And she couldn't love him. It was impossible.

All right, turn it around. Anna grabbed at the ridiculous. "You attacked Freddie because you were jealous."

That stopped him. He froze and blinked. "Jealous?"

"Yes, you couldn't bear to see me with another man. Nobody betrays you, Zach. Isn't that what you keep saying? To be betrayed you have to care."

He hadn't looked so stunned since she'd smacked him.

"Now what are you going to do to make it up to Freddie?"

"I already have." Murmured words, hardly heard.

"You have?"

"What?" Zach rubbed his hands over his neck. "Yes. I offered him a commission. Anna, why did you flaunt him?"

Back to the same topic. "Why did you overreact?"

Why had he? He knew. Now.

Seeing her with a boy, half naked. He could still feel the surge of fury. He had to stop Freddie from making the same mistake that he had. Couldn't he see she was poison? They were thoughts that buried the truth, because the truth hurt much more.

Another woman he cared for had betrayed him.

"My wife. My *ex*-wife."

Anna blinked.

Time to tell *her* the truth. Then it might dull the old pain burning in his chest.

"I never knew. I thought that we were perfect, that our life was perfect. I was rich and successful. So was she." He paused and stared down at the floor. "But I wasn't enough for her."

Anna's heart twisted at the pain in his voice. She didn't want to feel sorry for him. She didn't. But her feet moved her forward until she was so close that her hand reached out and took his. The warmth of contact made Zach meet her gaze.

"I found her. With a man who used to be my friend. Nathan Alexander. She was..." His eyes glittered and anger, bitterness burned there. "She had another man in her mouth."

"That's why you didn't—" Anna stopped more words.

His smile was wry. "Yes, a stupid overreaction, but then that's what I do best."

"No, it isn't."

"Anna..." He tilted her chin. "And then I saw you at that infamous Christmas party. You were so beautiful, so incredible. I thought that you... Well, it doesn't matter. I found you with Freddie. It was over.

"From then on, I regulated my relationships."

Anna's heart was pounding. "You wanted more?"

"Who wouldn't want you, Anna?"

The words caught a hitch in her chest.

"I'm sure every man you've slept with did."

She stood back from him. "You still don't believe me."

His hand slid over her jaw, her cheek, his thumb tracing over her mouth. Her skin prickled at his touch. There was a shadow to his gaze and it made Anna uneasy. He gave her a brief smile. "It doesn't matter. I would never expect to control anything you do."

Had he just, very politely, thrown her out of his life?

"Zach..."

"Hello? Mr. Quinn? The door was open!" David ran a hand over his windswept hair and stood in the kitchen doorway. His expression was neutral, but his gaze fixed on Zach alone. The awkwardness of the situation prickled over her skin. "I parked the car around the back, sir."

"Thank you, David." Zach gave him a tight smile. "Wait for us there, please."

"Yes, sir."

Anna let out an unconsciously held breath as Zach's chauffeur disappeared. "Well, we haven't much to take with us." She was already retreating back along the kitchen. She needed space from him. What he had said made no sense. And still he dismissed her attempts to share the truth with him.

"Anna."

"Zach." She waved back to the doorway and the stairs beyond. "I need to get dressed." She tugged at the belt so that it dug tight into her waist. "I want to get this over with. Move on."

He stared at her. "Move on?"

The edge to his voice hitched her breath in her throat. Damn it, the man confused her. "We're both tired. Our ride is here. We get ready. We leave."

"This isn't over."

His voice trailed after her. Anna gripped the banister and hauled herself up the narrow stairs. "Why do I feel like this will *never* be over?" she muttered.

ဆၣ

"Ready?"

Zach was waiting for her when she opened her bedroom door. There really was no escaping the man. It was a pity that Gregory, for all of his advance planning, hadn't thought to supply her with fresh clothing. An uncomfortable thought made her blush. Perhaps he had been planning on her not needing any.

She ran a hand over the shoulder strap of her dress. "Ready."

He stood back.

Letting out a nervous breath, Anna descended the stairs, shoes in hand. There was no sense in crippling herself yet. "Are you going to try to reason with Carl?"

Zach was a silent shadow behind her. His brooding quiet made her skin itch. Then his voice came from the darkness. "What would be the point?"

Anna stopped herself from turning and staring at him. There had been a spark of anger in his tone. Zach wanted to rile her. She would not give him the satisfaction. She knew with certainty now where their anger ended. No, she was not thinking about that.

Instead, she followed the labyrinth of doors to the small courtyard at the back of the house. Through the French doors, on the clean flags, sat Zach's Bentley, the engine ticking over.

Anna slipped on her shoes and winced against the cut of the leather into her bare feet.

"I thought you would have been used to them."

Anna went on ignoring him.

"You're Sophia's right hand. Attending everything that she had you organise. Or was it the fact that you weren't on your feet that much?"

"Have you finished?"

The door key was on the sill. She snatched it up. The chill morning wind whipped through the thinness of her dress and she shivered. She banged the door shut and locked it.

"No."

"What is your problem?"

"*You* have always been my problem."

She gave him a sharp smile. "Again. Snap."

The chauffeur stood beside the car, a door open. Zach waved for her to get inside. Anna pulled the seat belt over her chest and relaxed back into the cool leather. The door clunked shut. Anna closed her eyes. This was the old Zach, the Zach she was used to. There had been a brief twenty-four hour interlude of another man. Her mouth curled. Not exactly a *whole* day.

"So are you happy you won?" Zach clicked the seat belt. He stared straight ahead of him, his features a mask of stone.

Anna couldn't help looking at David. This was Zachary Quinn, possibly one of the most private men on the planet, and he was sniping at her in front of the staff. "Would the truth make any difference?"

Zach snorted. "It would be...novel."

"Did I miss something? Has today not happened?"

Zach ran a hand through his still damp hair. His attention had turned to the window, to the slow slide of the stone that marked the edge of the estate. "Wouldn't that be nice."

Anna's stared at the seat in front of her and ignored the pain that tightened in her chest. She didn't know him at all. It wasn't a lie when she said, "Yes."

She let her head fall back against the headrest.

Anna had promised herself that she would not regret her time with Zach.

Closing her eyes, the touch of his fingers, the slide of his skin over hers still prickled her body with awareness. No, she didn't regret it. How could she? The itch had been *properly* scratched. She shifted in her seat and was aware of Zach's gaze moving back to her. "What?"

"You sighed."

Had she?

"Well, I'd call it more than a sigh."

"Would you?"

He wasn't the only one who could be pigheaded.

"Anna..."

"What?"

Zach scrubbed at his face. "I'm being an idiot."

"Really?"

He cursed under his breath. "Fine."

She could feel his glare, goose bumps rising, but she would not look at him. He edged close and his breath stirred her too-sensitive skin. His voice was just above a harsh whisper, as if he suddenly remembered where he was. "I am contesting this will, Anna. Sofia will get nothing. And you?" He paused and heat melted through her at the almost touch of his lips over the shell of her ear. "You, you'll get what you deserve."

There was a sudden ache in her chest as her heart missed a beat.

She swallowed and willed herself to breathe normally.

Zach shifted back into his seat.

She risked a glance and found him staring out at the flash by of farmland. His face had set into the familiar hard mask.

You'll get what you deserve.

Was that a threat? Or a promise?

Chapter Twelve

"Good. You're here." Carl Petersen waved them out of the lift and towards his office.

"In one piece, you mean." Zach stood back from her. His deliberate distance was painful. Anna had to accept that there would be nothing more between them. And she should be relieved. She just wished there wasn't a burning hole in her chest.

The solicitor dabbed at his reddened forehead with a handkerchief. "That too." He stared back along the silent corridor and a pained expression crossed his face. "There are more forfeits."

She winced at the run of Zach's cursing. "What now?"

Carl handed her a letter with Gregory's familiar scrawl. Despite the games he was playing with her life, she couldn't stop her fingers running over her name. Her throat tightened. Anna closed her eyes and took a deep, calming breath.

"Anna?"

The brief touch of Zach's fingertips on her bare shoulder shot her eyes open. "It's nothing." Quickly, she tore open the envelope, pulled out a thick, folded piece of paper and scanned its contents. She thought about using some of Zach's more colourful curses. "Where is she?"

"She's camped in my office." Carl flushed at his choice of words. Anna felt sorry for the man, Gregory was stressing his life too.

"Thank you." Anna handed him the letter and straightened her spine. "I suppose it is time."

"What?" Zach's hand closed around her arm. The heat of his touch prickled her skin. Anna willed herself to ignore it. "Who?"

She pulled her arm free. "Gregory wants me to have a chat with his wife."

"This is beyond ridiculous."

"I have to follow Mr. Brabant's wishes." Carl winced. "As...uncomfortable...as they have become."

"If this is what he wants..." She lifted her shoulders and started the long walk to Carl's office. *Gregory, you are insane. You really are.* She stopped before the closed door and made her hand move to the cold doorknob. It twisted.

"This is completely stupid!" Sofia declared, waving a thick sheet of cream paper at her sister. "'You have something to say to me?' And that buffoon of a solicitor said Gregory was in his right mind. Right mind my—"

"Sofia." Anna closed the door. She willed her hand to let go of the doorknob. "Carl's just doing his job."

Sofia muttered something foul and flopped into a chair. She pulled at a strand of her long, blonde hair and stared at it. "He orders me, *me* here at this Godforsaken hour. You'll have to apologise to Sean. I'll miss his appointment now. The man will dye my hair green next time he sees me."

Anna let out a slow breath and allowed her sister to rant. Sofia was unapproachable before noon on any day of the week.

But Saturday, it wasn't worth your eardrums tackling her before three. "Gregory left me a note too."

"And it said what?" Sofia launched herself out of the chair and headed for the arrangement of glasses and bottles on a cabinet. She lifted a bottle and glared at the label. "You'd think he'd have something of better quality to offer his clients. He charges enough."

All right, she had to follow Gregory's instructions. Time to untangle the lies.

"I reacted on instinct." Anna slipped her feet out of her stupid sandals and curled her toes into the deep carpet. "I thought it would stop me getting too close to him. I trusted Isabelle. I thought she was a friend. Turns out she was more *your* friend."

Sofia twisted off the bottle cap and poured the water into a tumbler. "What are you rambling about? You're worse than Carl."

"She told me that Zach liked virgins." Anna didn't miss the smirk that briefly touched her sister's lips. "Her idea. Or yours?"

"His." She sipped her water and turned to face her. "I know about his little *problem* with women. He prefers lack of sexual experience in a partner so they will never know—"

"Stop." Anger curled tight in her gut. "Stop the lies now."

Sofia smiled around her glass. "So touchy about him, Anna. But then you always have been."

"So you thought you'd give my idiocy a hand."

"I thought that you wanted to have some fun," Sofia said, settling herself back into her chair. She crossed her legs and twitched her skirt over her knee. "That you'd stopped being a silly frump. You just needed a little push."

"A push?" Anna moved forward. Her body felt awkward, years of Sofia's put-downs tightening every muscle. But Gregory was right. The words of his letter repeated in her head.

You want to escape? Then stop pretending to be something you never have been. See Sofia. It seems neither of you could see sense over this.

"Without your help, I would have seen sense earlier, stopped—"

"And you can stop blaming me, Anna." Her gaze flicked over her body. "You're a grown woman. So, I had fun spreading a few rumours about you. So what? That people believed them has always amazed me."

Sofia was right.

She had been too much of a coward. Afraid of pulling away, of blaming everything on her sister's tight grip. She was right...but that didn't mean that what Sofia had done was right. "You didn't have fun, Sofia. It was spiteful." She stopped in front of her and watched as Sofia ran a taloned fingertip around the rim of the glass. The action threw her mind back to the bar, to Nathan. Heat fired through her face. "You." She swallowed the raw taste of bile. "You pushed all those odious men at me. I spend most of my time at any event fighting off your friends."

Sofia shrugged. "In the beginning. But then your reputation ran ahead of itself." Her laughter grated against Anna's stretched nerves. "Men couldn't wait to unwrap those conservative layers."

"Why?"

Sofia shrugged. "Beats me."

The familiar burn of dislike, of disappointment, soured her gut. It was time to face her sister as an adult. "Why would you think it fun to let everyone think your sister was a slut?"

The smirk faded from her face and her expression became stone. Anna felt the hairs prickle on the back of her neck. "I wanted you to know how it felt."

Anna blinked. "Excuse me?"

Sofia stood and Anna willed herself not to step back. "Poor little Anna." Her voice was a whine. "Poor little Anna who lost her mother, her father." Her skin had flushed and the grip on her glass had her knuckles white. "Everyone coddled you. Gregory, especially Gregory, even Zach. But me?" Her voice was thick and Anna thought she saw the reddening shine of tears in her eyes. "What about me?"

"You?"

Sofia turned away. "Me. I lost no one, obviously. I was nineteen. I was an adult. I didn't lose a mother, a father I worshipped."

"Sofia..." Anna rested her hand on her sister's stiff shoulder. Sofia yanked herself free.

"I don't need your sympathy."

"You resent me."

Her laugh was bitter. "Oh, you're so *understanding*, Anna." Sofia turned back to her and the familiar mocking twist had returned to her features. "I played you because I could."

"And now you have everything you wanted." Anna ran her fingers through her untidy hair, scrunching the ends in tight fists. "You have the house, you have Zach's business."

"Do I?"

Anna stared at her. "Well, you told Carl I was with Freddie. We broke the terms Gregory set."

Sofia drained her glass and banged it back down onto the cabinet. "I'm sure you can find somewhere else to live after today, Anna." She picked up her bag and slung it over her shoulder. "You always fall on your feet. You'll do it again."

"Is this all that Gregory asked of you?"

"It's all I'm giving to this charade." She tugged open the door. Zach strode into the room. "She's all yours."

"Sofia..." Anna didn't know what to say. Her sister was walking out on her. There was the sudden grief of knowing the sister she could have had, of that life lost to her.

The woman stalked down the long corridor without a backward glance.

"Anna, what did she say?"

The concern in Zach's eyes was just a mockery. She slipped on her protecting social smile. "Let's get this over with."

He frowned and Anna ignored him.

She'd meant what she'd said about Middleton. It was beautiful, but it wasn't real. She couldn't recreate the happiness she had found there as a child. She'd been foolish to believe that she could. It was a dream. Nothing more.

Anna had her savings. She had contacts. A job and a new place to live, that was her plan for the future.

And Zach? She had no clue and she had to ignore the tight pain fixed in her chest. From what he had said she was foolish to try to push further.

She focused on Carl, instead, watching him neatly arrange his papers over his desk.

He twitched a smile at her. "I have everything I need to discuss with you here."

"What is there to discuss?" Zach closed the door. "We broke the agreement. Everything goes to Sofia."

Carl winced. "Not...exactly." He looked back to his desk. "Can we sit?"

Zach's hand briefly touched the small of Anna's back and it jolted her forward. She sank into the same chair she had sat in only twenty-four hours before. The leather was cold against her skin and she shivered. "Tell us the worst of it, Mr. Petersen. What else could I have lost?"

She knew Zach was staring at her. Again, she ignored him.

"You lasted...fifteen hours." Carl Petersen flicked through his papers and pulled out more handwritten envelopes that Anna had seen on his desk the day before. "One for each of you." He stood, his reddened face flushing further. "And I'm sorry, these have to be read in private."

Zach stared at him. "That's it? Yet more envelopes?"

Colour still slashed the solicitor's cheeks. "Mr. Brabant's will has caused trouble to a number of people. I'm sorry. But I believe these letters will explain everything. My instructions are to leave you to read them."

He left, the door closing with an overloud thump in the thick silence of his office.

Anna stared at the front of the envelope and traced over Gregory's familiar scrawl. What was he playing at now? Her hand trembled and she turned the envelope over and tore it open.

She read.

And closed her eyes in disbelief. Her heart thudded.

It was over.

"This was just a game?" Fury lined Zach's voice and he threw the letter onto the desk. "I get the company. You get your cottage. And his parting line? 'Zach, get your head out of your arse'."

Anna couldn't help the spluttered laugh. "Sounds like Gregory." Her humour faded. This was it. They could go their separate ways. It was for the best. Wasn't it? "Well..." Damn, her bag was in Zach's apartment and that meant she didn't have the keys to her car parked in the basement. But there was no way on earth she was going to ask him for them. "I have to be going."

Zach's head snapped up. "No."

"This has finished." She waved her letter at him. "Mine says the same thing." Her mouth twitched. "Without the arse comment."

He frowned. "This is far from over, Anna."

The familiar spark of anger ignited in her gut. "I won't do this anymore."

"We have to—"

"What?" Anna pushed back her chair with a rough scrape over the thick carpet. "I...I need to get on with my life."

"So you're running again?"

Anna pulled on her sandals. She would have to ask Carl for a loan. Her cheeks burned at the thought. She was supposed to be living a new life and that meant being an adult and not being afraid. She took a deep breath. "My car keys and purse are in your apartment. If you wouldn't mind giving me a lift, please?"

Zach stared at her.

"All that I have right now is the clothes I'm standing up in. So is that a yes?"

With a look of disbelief on his face, he waved his arm towards the door. "Yes."

They startled Carl who was hovering outside of his office. He gave a small smile and pushed his glasses back onto the bridge of his nose. "I'm sorry. I couldn't reveal the truth to you, not even to Mrs. Brabant."

"Sofia knows?" Her anger finally made sense to Anna. She had thought that everything would fall to her. And now, for all of Sofia's scheming, she had none of it.

"Yes."

Zach's short laugh was harsh. "Gregory hasn't left us with any more tricks, has he?"

"No, Mr. Quinn."

Carl held out his hand to Anna. "Well, good luck, Ms. Shrewsbury."

She forced herself to smile and take his hand. "Thank you. In some ways, you must be glad we didn't last the week."

He snorted. "I suppose you could say that."

He shook Zach's hand and disappeared back into his office. There was a heavy and relieved sigh just before the door thumped shut.

"You wanted that lift?"

"Yes, thank you."

Awkwardness itched over her. They no longer had any reason to stay in each other's company. And really, for both their sakes, staying far, far away from each other was probably the most sensible thing to do. That's what the rational part of her mind was declaring. She clung to it, because that thought helped her ignore the pain twisting her insides.

They were silent in the lift as it slowly juddered back down to the basement.

And just as silent in the slow ride back to Zach's apartment.

Zach let her precede him into the long hallway. Her heels clicked over the walnut flooring and Anna forced her mind to focus, not to slip back to the night before. She headed straight for the study and found her handbag. Her overnight bag still sat there too.

"Mind if I change?"

Zach shrugged out of his jacket. "Go ahead."

"Thank you."

A muscle in his cheek jumped.

Anna's sudden politeness was excruciating.

Zach threw his jacket over a chair and found himself in the kitchen. He was still having trouble processing what Gregory had done. And how much the old man had known. About him, at least. But it was over. He had his business. Anna had her house. And they could walk away...

...when her test proved negative.

His heart kicked.

What had he been thinking?

Zach stared, sightless, out of the long kitchen window. He hadn't been thinking. He didn't do that when Anna was involved. He reacted. In lust and in fury. He ran a hand through his hair and pushed himself away from the kitchen counter. His eyes burned with tiredness. He couldn't remember the last time he had slept.

No, that was a lie. He had slept with his arms wrapped around Anna's warm body and the herbal scent of her hair following him into the deepest sleep he'd ever experienced.

Zach cursed. "Tired thoughts." He would tell David to drive her back to her car and then hit his bed. He remembered his biology lessons. It would be over a week before Anna's body would produce the hormone for which the pregnancy kit tested.

Zach closed his eyes. And didn't that sound dispassionate? He wished it felt that way, because his gut was in a knot at the thought of having created a new life with Anna. He had never considered having children and he was certain she hadn't.

Neither of them were designed to be parents.

He told himself that and a single memory from his childhood burned beneath it.

Seeing his father's face when Zach's mother, looking so beautiful she almost glowed, had disappeared into the night. He had been five years old and the conversation still haunted him.

"Why don't you think Mummy looked beautiful?"

His father stroked his hand over Zach's hair and it trembled. "She did. She does. It's just not for me."

His father had smiled, the bright and mischievous grin reserved solely for him, and picked Zach up. He could still feel the tight, almost desperate strength of his father's hold. He blinked and Zach had thought it odd. It seemed as though his father had tears in his eyes.

A few days later, the tabloids splashed her first infidelity across the country.

His life was never the same again.

Zach let go of a slow breath.

No, he and Anna should not be parents.

"So...I'll get a taxi back."

He jumped. He hadn't heard her come into the kitchen. "David can take you."

"I don't want to impose—"

"No." He held up his hand. "Enough politeness for one lifetime, please."

Anna was staring at him. "Then I won't say thank you."

She lifted her bag, slung it over her shoulder and turned. Anna was leaving.

He had tried to offer her more, to accept her for who she was and she had turned away. The familiar fury lashed up through him, commanding him to throw harsh words after her, to stop his own pain by hurting her. "So you're going back to your old life?"

"There never was my 'old life', Zach. It's something you'll never believe of me."

He stalked toward her and the fire burned in her dark eyes. Her chin lifted.

He stopped. "So all of those men lied?"

"For Sofia, yes."

"That's insane."

Anna's mouth twisted into a sharp smile. "Hello? You've met my sister." She jabbed her thumb at the open doorway. "I have to go."

More anger rose and again he wanted to make her hurt the way he did... But fury didn't work. It had never worked yet. Zach forced those words back and offered one that had escaped before. "Stay."

Anna froze. "Why?"

"Why?" He blinked.

Why?

He wanted her. From that first stolen kiss, he had wanted *her...*

"See? I don't play your games anymore. I've been an idiot for the past six years. But now I'm free." She readjusted the weight of her overnight bag. "Free of Sofia and of you."

"Damn it, Anna, why are we denying this attraction?" His hand stroked her neck and her responding shiver fed back through his fingers. "You can't have already forgotten how good we were."

Anna stepped back from him. "Would we have to strike a deal? Would I have to agree to an exclusivity clause again?"

Zach worked the muscles in his jaw. That particular conversation burned fresh in his memory too. Isabelle's actions had demanded that he protect himself...but the request had only met with horror from Anna. Her look of disgust still seared him. It was the same with all the women in his life.

One man could never be enough.

With Anna, he finally had to accept it.

"No," he said.

Anna swallowed and her throat ached with unshed tears.

He didn't care.

They would simply use each other for sex. And he wouldn't care where she was when it wasn't her allotted time to be with him. Nor with whom. Damn him. "So you don't mind, that of course when it isn't your turn, that I'm sleeping with Nathan, with Eric." Her smile was sharp. "Maybe even old Sir Nigel, who seemed quite keen on the idea last night." Her head tilted. "And naturally, for your precious privacy, I'll be ultra discreet."

Colour cut across his cheeks, but the rest of his face could have been carved from stone. "No. I don't mind."

Bile rose to her mouth and her stomach turned. "Sir Nigel Wallingham? Twenty stone of gristled old man, heaving and panting—"

"For Christ's sake, Anna, what more do you want from me?"

Anna stared at him.

He straightened, ran a hand over his hair. The calm, controlled Zach had returned. "I don't need to know the details." A bitter smile twisted his mouth. "I don't *want* to know them."

"And you'd be happy with this arrangement?"

"Yes."

"Really?"

"What the hell are you pushing for, Anna? I've agreed. Deal done."

Anna closed her eyes.

Zach wanted her and the deal was tempting. She held down a sour laugh, even as harshly as he had offered that deal. Yet, who he thought she was still stabbed at her. Anna knew that the more time she spent with Zach, the more she would be unable to deny her feelings. She didn't want to think about the time when he would simply terminate his deal once he was sated. To save herself, she could have only one answer.

"No."

"No?" He stared at the floor. "What else do you want? For everyone to know?" More blood flushed his face and when he looked back to her the bitter defeat in his eyes shocked her. "All right. I'll agree to that, too."

"Oh my God." A hysterical laugh burst out of her. "You mean it."

He jerked a nod.

This was Zach, a man scarred by his wife's infidelities, her lies, a man who shrouded himself in privacy.

What the hell was he doing? Damn him, she knew...

"Oh, this is another of your games. I accept and you laugh in my face."

"Am I laughing now?"

His lips brushed hers in a swift caress. Pressing harder, his mouth held her and the familiar taste of him had her heart pounding. His hands slipped over her cheek, her jaw and she couldn't help herself. She opened her mouth to him.

The meeting of hot tongues released a moan. Hers or his, she couldn't tell.

Heat surged and she deepened the kiss. She stumbled back, hit a cupboard and cursed the awkward shape of her bag as the impact dragged her mouth from his.

Anna stared into his darkened eyes. The heat, the desire there, fuelled her need.

"You want me."

"Any way I can get you."

Her breath caught. "And you mean that, too."

Zach sighed. "Anna." He stepped back and she missed the warmth of his body. "I want you." His smile was wry. "For six years, I've wanted you." He turned away and Anna watched him pace over the tiled floor. "I never understood how Gregory, nor my father could live the way they did. Live with how their wives behaved."

He smiled, something almost sad. "I know that you have to be the woman you are." His hand rubbed over his jaw and he closed his eyes.

Anna stared at him. What was he saying? He had said something similar only a few hours before...

His eyes opened and what she saw there stopped her heart.

"As long as you come back to me, I can live with that."

Emotion choked her. A tear ran cold down her cheeks.

Betrayal had scarred him and yet he was willing to publicly share her.

"Zach." Her hand pressed against his chest and the solid thud of his heart beat through her palm. "Thank you for the offer of letting me be with other men. But I *don't* want it."

Silent, he turned away from her and Anna's fingers drew back into her palm.

"I didn't lie, Zach. There has been only you." She was talking to his back. "Why don't you want to believe that?"

His laugh was bitter. "So you lied for six years?" He leant against the kitchen counter and regarded her with cool eyes. "Why do something that stupid?"

Anna winced. She did deserve that one. She *had* been stupid. Sucking in courage, she pulled her bag back over her head and dropped it to the floor. He had been honest. And from a man like Zach, his offer had been incredible. It was time for her to be just as honest.

"You scared me."

He blinked.

She rubbed at dry lips, her mouth suddenly parched by nerves. "The lies started early. I didn't come here"—she waved her hand around the bright kitchen—"to this apartment because I thought you weren't in it." Her smile was strained in his continued silence. "I knew you'd be here. Made certain. I came for you."

"For me?"

"You'd just turned my world upside down, Zach. I was still full of Isabelle's little jibes about you. But I had to risk it, in spite of her warnings."

"You ran."

"I thought what she had warned me about was all true."

"And letting me think you'd slept with most of the country? Simply going with the opposite of my need for virgins?"

Heat bled into her cheeks. She had never thought she would be explaining this to him, and worse, wanting him to understand. "That, and my reputation would be so terrible..."

"...I wouldn't touch you?"

Anna nodded.

"Well it worked. Mostly." His expression was wry. "Except for my constant need to find another wall to push you up against."

"That wasn't just your need."

Zach's hands stopped rubbing over his face. "So we're in agreement about this mutual lust thing?"

Lust.

Was he closing down on her? Retreating?

As long as you come back to me...

The words tightened her gut. Lust could not make a man say that.

Anna closed the distance between them. She tried not to see the tremble in her hands as her fingers closed around his and drew them tight into her own. She swallowed.

And said it.

"I love you."

Zach simply stared at her.

Yes, it was official. She was insane. But there was no going back. She had said it in the cold light of day. There were no excuses of being half asleep now.

Now if only he'd say something. *Anything.*

"You love me?"

Panic fired through her blood and she wanted to run. Something in his tone sounded...wrong. Her breath stopped and she knew she was waiting for his harsh burst of laughter.

"You love me."

Zach pulled his hands free and strode out of the kitchen.

ॐ

His hand shook as he splashed brandy into a glass.

He'd gulped a mouthful before he realised what he was doing. He grimaced and stared into the dark liquid. The brandy burned his gut.

He had offered her everything he thought she wanted. Everything. At that moment, he hadn't cared about anything else other than having Anna in his life. Any way he could. Something inside of him had cracked when she turned him down. But then she had said...

The thought burst the same panic through him and his hand tightened around the glass.

Anna loved him.

ञकओ

Anna stared at her hands, the burn of his touch still on her skin. "All right." She drew in a much-needed breath. "Not the response I was expecting." She made herself follow his path out of the kitchen. "But better than laughter. Just."

She found Zach in his drawing room.

Unwanted, her mind flipped back to the night she had entered his home with stolen keys. He stood before his drinks cabinet, a crystal tumbler already half empty of brandy. Light from the window cut sharp across his profile, shone through his dark tousled hair. He really was beautiful.

Her heart hammered, as fast as when she had stood in the same spot six years before. She half expected him to turn and have his old fury burst back over her. Fury. She had never questioned it before. She did now. "You told me to get out, that night. Why?"

Zach straightened his shoulders, put down the glass and turned. "All that I could think about was you and the fact that I'd almost had you at the Christmas party." He laughed, something bitter, tired. "Me. The man who was so controlled, so private. I'd nearly made a fool of myself. Again." He glanced back to the glass, toyed with the rim, but didn't pick it up again. "And then you came to me."

A smile lurked on his mouth and the promise there pooled heat low in her pelvis. Was he remembering them? It drew her to him. He caressed her jaw, slow, exploring, and her heart squeezed. His thumb stroked over her bottom lip.

The gentle kiss swept warmth down to her toes.

"I forgot everything in you." His forehead pressed against hers and the intimate gesture forced a sigh. "Wanted everything. Until Freddie."

Anna closed her eyes and guilt crawled up her spine. "I'm sorry."

"No." His lips brushed over one eyelid and then the other. "I was an idiot. I offered money. I protect myself with money."

More kisses traced over her jaw, edging back towards her mouth. "What are we doing here, Zach?"

"What we've been doing since yesterday?"

Anna couldn't help the smile. "Yes, I got that part." She willed herself to pull back. "With us." She held his darkened gaze. "I meant what I said. And *you* ran."

He sighed. "I know. It just wasn't what I was expecting. You turned me down again. And again." The slight smile faded. Anna's stomach dropped. Had she made yet another stupid mistake? His hand slipped over her shoulder, gently stroking her arm, and then he pulled her to him. His arms enfolded her and she drew his warm, familiar scent deep into her lungs.

"I want to say it now, so it's not misconstrued...later." There was a smirk in his voice before he kissed her hair. "We'll fight, Anna. We'll scream and shout. We can't help ourselves." He sighed. "I love you. Probably have for a long time. But I needed Gregory to point it out."

"We both did."

Zach's hand slid down the smoothness of her jersey, resting possessively on her hip. "Where were we?"

"Can you say it again?"

"What? Misconstrued?"

Her fist dug hard into his ribs and he grunted. "You know what I want to hear, Mr. Quinn."

"Fighting?"

Anna bit back a smile. She pulled out of his hold and took his hand in hers. "Going to make you say it," she said.

"Is that a dare, Anna?"

She glared at him. "Careful, Zach, I might have to enforce the exclusivity clause."

"Ah, you've begun the negotiations..." His grin was wicked and her heart did a little kick.

Anna couldn't stop her smirk and she all but dragged him from the drawing room. "Oh yes, serious negotiations."

"It is possible that they could go on for days?"

"There'll need to be a thorough investigation...I'll have to go into detail."

Zach burst out laughing. "But only if I'm a very good boy?"

Anna stopped at the door to his bedroom. She held out her other hand and Zach took it. His grip was warm, strong and Anna felt the flutter in her chest. She was allowed to love him. And he returned her love. That still simply didn't feel real.

She smiled. "Honestly, Zach...I'm not lying anymore. There is only you. No one else."

"I know." He opened the door. The sheets spilled out over the bed, the floor and the scent of them still lingered. "Fresh room?"

Anna laughed. "Would be nice."

He pulled her along the hall to the next bedroom. Closing the door, he leant back against it. Light filtered through the thin-curtained windows and shadowed his face. Anna couldn't stop her need to trace over the smile that curved his mouth, sighing when he kissed her fingertips.

He tucked a loose strand of hair behind her ear, the slow contact sending more shivers over her skin. "I believe you, Anna. I do. It's just...we wasted so much time." He winced. "I will always regret that."

"No regrets, Zach. I promised myself." She smiled. "And I'm sure Gregory didn't orchestrate all of this for us to spend our time feeling stupid."

His laughter sounded warm, real. "No. We can't waste his efforts."

He pushed himself away from the door.

Heat flooded Anna's body at the predatory smile curving Zach's mouth. She found herself backing away, until her legs hit the bed and she dropped to the deep mattress.

"I believe you were going to make me say something?"

She stared up at him. Her mouth twitched. "I was?"

"Anna..." The low growl to his voice pulsed through her blood.

"You may have to..." Her words dried.

"...remind you?" He flicked open a button and then another. Warm skin slid into view, until he shrugged out of his shirt and dropped it to the floor.

Zach getting naked for her.

She could get very used to that.

Anna stopped his hands on his belt buckle. "Say it, Zach."

His chest rose and fell with a slow breath.

The smooth run of very biteable muscle... Anna unconsciously wet her lips.

Zach grinned.

He knelt before her, his hands sliding up the sleek cotton of her trousers, easing her legs apart. She swallowed and suddenly it was hard to breathe. The clean scent of his skin tantalised her. His thumbs pressed against her inner thighs, heat surged and she fought down the very real need to squirm.

Closer.

"Anna Shrewsbury..."

The hot pulse of his voice dropped passion into her blood. Her lips parted. His mouth was only inches from hers. If she just tilted her head to the left...

"I love you."

She bit her lip to lessen the swift pain in her chest. It hurt. The joy hurt.

Oh God.

Zach loved her.

"Anna?"

She wiped hard at a stupid tear. "This is real, isn't it? We're real. *Us.*"

"Oh yes. And I promise, we'll be real for quite some time." Zach's clever fingers slid across her pelvis and he grinned as she yelped. "Now. I've met your demand." His grin was sly. "So, do with me what you will."

Her finger traced a slow path over his pectoral, slipping lower, lower... "Oh, I intend to." Anna matched his grin. "Starting now."

About the Author

Kim Rees started writing when she was ten years old. That's...okay we'll not go into how long ago that was now. But in 2002, she gave in and started writing romance...well...sex. To her surprise, it came naturally. Yes. Please groan at the pun.

Kim lives halfway between Strawberry Fields and Penny Lane. Honest. Just *please* don't ask her to sing...

To learn more about Kim, please visit www.romancefiction.co.uk. Send an email to Kim at kim@romancefiction.co.uk or join her Yahoo! group to join in the fun with other readers as well as Kim! http://groups.yahoo.com/group/daughtersofcirce.

Look for these titles

It was nothing personal, just a business arrangement.

Nothing Personal
© 2007 Jaci Burton

Ryan McKay is a multi-millionaire with a problem. He needs a bride to fulfill the terms of his grandfather's will. Unfortunately, the one he chose just bailed on him and he's hours away from losing his company. Enter Faith Lewis—his demure, devoted assistant. Ryan convinces Faith to step in and marry him, assuring her their marriage is merely a business deal. Ryan is certain he can keep this strictly impersonal. After all, he's the product of a loveless marriage and for years has sealed his own heart in an icy stone. Despite Faith's warmth, compassion and allure, he's convinced he's immune to her charms.

Faith will do anything for her boss, but—marry him? The shy virgin sees herself as plain and unattractive, a product of a bitter mother who drummed into her head that she wasn't worthy of a man's love. But she agrees to help Ryan fulfill the terms of his grandfather's will, hoping she doesn't lose her heart to him in the process.

But love rarely listens to logic, and what follows is anything but business.

Available now in ebook and print from Samhain Publishing.

An instant family wasn't what David had planned for his life, but once he met single mother Lucy he knew he had to change his plans.

The Whole Shebang
© 2007 Elisa Adams

Fifth grade teacher David Storm has had it up to *here* with one of his students. Lately the boy's attitude has changed. He's is obnoxious and rowdy, unable to sit still for five seconds, and is constantly interrupting to ask questions that have nothing to do with the subjects they're studying. The boy's twin brother is just the opposite—so quiet that it has David worried. He calls their mother and tells her he needs to speak with her, setting in motion a whole set of events he never could have imagined.

Lucy Parker knows what her boys are trying to do—and she doesn't approve. Since her divorce from their father three years ago, the eleven-year-olds have been trying to set her up with every single man in the tri-county area. They mean well, but she isn't looking for love. She's got enough trouble raising four rambunctious boys, and she doesn't need to add someone else to the list. Especially not their latest choice—their very handsome yet way-too-young-for-her teacher.

Available now in ebook and print from Samhain Publishing.

GREAT
cheap
fun

Discover eBooks!
THE FASTEST WAY TO GET THE HOTTEST NAMES

Get your favorite authors on your favorite reader, long before they're
out in print! Ebooks from Samhain go wherever you go, and work with
whatever you carry—Palm, PDF, Mobi, and more.

Samhain
Publishing, ltd

WWW.SAMHAINPUBLISHING.COM

Printed in the United States
100199LV00002B/103-108/A